The Once and Future King

T. H. White

Curriculum Unit

Thomas Bondra

D1211621

 The Center for Learning

Thomas J. Bondra received his M.A. in media studies at the New School for Social Research, N.Y. A world literature and communications instructor whose experience includes teaching at St. John's College, Portsmouth, England, he has participated in a summer Shakespeare institute and studied contemporary Arthurian literature under a fellowship program.

The Publishing Team

Rose Schaffer, M.A., President/Chief Executive Officer
Bernadette Vetter, M.A., Vice President
Diane Podnar, M.S., Managing Editor
Amy Richards, M.A., Editorial Director

List of credits found on Acknowledgments page beginning on 119.

ISBN 1-56077-287-5

Contents

Introduction

The figure of Arthur, the Once and Future King, has, for centuries, engaged the imagination of men and women. The legends say the mortally wounded Arthur was taken away to the isle of Avalon to heal his wounds and to sleep until the time he is needed once again. Throughout the centuries, he has been awakened, from time to time, when people needed an ideal, a hero. He was awakened by Thomas Malory when the old feudal order was being replaced by the Renaissance in England. He was awakened by Alfred, Lord Tennyson, in the nineteenth century, when beliefs were challenged by Darwin, Marx, and Freud. He was awakened in the 1960s when American leaders were being gunned down in the streets.

What is it about the story of Arthur, his wife Guenever, his best friend Lancelot, and the enchanter Merlyn that has enchanted readers again and again over the centuries? It is a story of hungering for an ideal that is doomed to fail because of human weaknesses. It is at the same time a true-to-life experience and an expression of a higher ideal that makes T.H. White's account of the story of Arthur one of the most popular modern retellings.

Written between 1938 and 1952, T.H. White's *The Once and Future King* has remained, for most modern readers, the definitive account of Arthur who tries to put into practice what Merlyn taught him, only to be frustrated at every turn by human frailty.

Not only does White's novel present characters with which students can identify, he also addresses concerns which are on their minds. In an age of nuclear arms, Whites's thematic discussion of war and peace, of *homo ferox*, ferocious man, and of the lessons to be learned from our fellow creatures in the planet, have even more urgency than they did when they were written.

Introducing students to T.H. White's *The Once and Future King* will not only awaken Arthur from his sleep, in their lives, but also awaken the ideal in their hearts.

Teacher Notes

T.H. White's *The Once and Future King* is a long, complex work of literature. A teacher who would like to use this work as part of a course could not possibly hope to cover the entire novel in depth within normal class time limits. These lessons, then, are not intended to exhaust the depth of this novel, but are merely an attempt to aid the student in reading the book and selecting important themes and techniques.

This series of ten lessons is designed to help the student understand the novel. Consequently, the lessons are presented sequentially from Book One, "The Sword in the Stone" through Book Four, "The Candle in the Wind." These are not meant to be "single class" lessons, but may take anywhere from two or three to four or five classes depending on the time the teacher wishes to spend on the novel. The sequential arrangement of the lessons may also help the teacher who wishes to assign only part of the novel. For example, only "The Sword in the Stone" could be assigned and only lessons one, two, and three used.

If the entire novel has already been read by the students as a summer reading assignment or part of an independent reading program, a teacher may wish to group various lessons thematically rather than sequentially. For example, lessons three, five, and seven discuss the development and decline of Arthur's ideal of "Might for Right" and could be taught as a unit.

The lessons emphasize four major topics: (1) The place of *The Once and Future King* within the context of Arthurian legends, "The Matter of Britain," as a whole and in particular its relationship with Malory's *Le Morte D'Arthur* (Lessons 1, 2, 3, 9); (2) The thematic development of Arthur's ideal of "Might for Right" and White's views concerning war (Lessons 3, 5, 7, 8); (3) a look at how White creates believable, psychologically deep, three-dimensional characters (Lessons 4, 6); (4) an attempt to broaden students' understanding of the novel beyond the literary into a wider, humanities base (Lesson 10).

A teacher should feel free to use those lessons which are more appropriate to the context in which the novel is taught. In a survey course, the emphasis may be on placing the novel in a larger literary context; in a genre course, the focus may be to adapt to many different uses in the classroom.

In addition to the ten lessons, there is a special section of supplementary materials which includes a series of objective reading-check quizzes for each of the four books of the novel. The two larger books ("The Sword in the Stone" and "The Ill-Made Knight") each have two quizzes. A final test on the entire book has been designed to be taken after the lessons are completed. This is a combination objective and short essay test which asks students to synthesize the material. A series of reading-check questions are intended to prevent the slower student from getting lost in the reading of the novel. Finally, there is a bibliography to aid both teacher and students. It contains entries of source materials, research materials, and other modern retellings of the Arthurian legends for further reading.

The legends of Arthur, Guenever, and Lancelot have spoken to human beings for the last fourteen hundred years. They are stories which are grounded in our own hopes and dreams and in our own faults and frailties. This book helps us to discover that Arthur truly is not dead, but inside each of us waiting to be awakened. Arthur is truly *The Once and Future King*.

Values

1. The need for education to mold a person's character

2. The need to curb an inclination for destruction

3. The importance of being true to one's self

4. The need for an ideal to shape the purpose and meaning of lives

5. The need to continue to pursue the ideal despite all setbacks

6. The understanding of the imperfections of human nature

7. The need to accept the consequences of one's actions

Lesson 1
The Matter of Britain

Objectives
- To establish what is already known about the Arthurian legends
- To show how the legends of Arthur have grown and changed over the last 1300 years
- To show that many variations of heroic legends develop over time

Notes to the Teacher

Most students have already had some exposure to the legends of King Arthur through films, television, or previous reading. What they may be unaware of, however, is that the stories of King Arthur and his knights have a long, varied history that is not only tied up in the history of England, but also in the histories and cultures of many other countries.

These stories of love, adventure, spiritual longing, and the belief in an ideal which transcends humanity's faults and frailties, have been used over hundreds of years in many different cultures to give hope to many people. *The Once and Future King* is only one of many versions of the stories of Arthur, Lancelot, Guenever, and Merlyn.

It is important that students recognize this fact. They are bound to come across discrepancies between what they think they know about the legend and the version presented by White. They should be able to recognize these discrepancies and discuss why they exist. They should recognize that even among themselves, although they recognize certain common elements of the legend, their version of certain characters and events has been colored by the sources they remember. The Arthur of *Excalibur*, the film, is quite different from the Arthur of *Camelot*, the musical.

The purpose of this lesson is to show students that many variations of a heroic legend can exist and continue to develop in many different countries for many different reasons.

Procedure
1. Distribute **Handout 1** and let students fill it in quickly. This should be followed by a classroom discussion in which students share their responses. The teacher should be ready to point out discrepancies.

2. Distribute **Handout 2**, part 1. From classroom discussion, students should reach a consensus on the essential elements of the Arthurian legend in the four areas on the handout.

3. **Handout 2**, part 2, can be assigned as homework or as individual work. It asks the student to demonstrate how these same essential elements in the Arthur stories can also be found in one other hero story. The teacher may want to ask the class for names of other heroes and list them on the board. Students can then choose one name from the list and use it to complete the assignment. These could be from other literature which they have read (Beowulf, Ulysses, Roland) or from "pop culture." The results of this assignment can be shared in small groups or with the class.

4. Distribute **Handout 3** to review the geography and history of Britain and its neighbors. This could be done as a library research project: finding places in an atlas and discussing their significance; assigning each student one place to report on; discussing the material if it has already been covered in another class.

5. Using the experience and knowledge from **Handouts 1** and **3**, students can use **Handout 4** to see when and where various elements of the Arthurian legend have arisen. Emphasize important changes and developments of the legend, NOT the names and dates. Point out the importance of Malory in the development of the legend and as an influence on White.

Name_____

Date_____

A Personal Arthurian Inventory

Directions: Answer the following questions in preparation for class discussion.

1. In what ways do you remember having heard about the story of King Arthur (childhood books, comics, films, cartoons, television shows, books, plays, etc.)? Give any titles that you can remember.

2. What things do you remember about the story of King Arthur?

3. Can you identify:

    1. The Sword in the Stone

    2. Camelot

    3. The Round Table

    4. Lancelot

    5. Guenever

    6. Excalibur

    7. Morgan La Fay

    8. Mordred

    9. The Holy Grail

    10. Merlyn

4. What meaning does the story of King Arthur have for you?

5. What other things about the story of King Arthur would you like to learn more about?

Creating a Myth

Part 1

Directions: Read the following and reach a consensus on the Arthurian legend.

1. Mysterious Origins—Where does he come from?

2. Superhuman Deeds—What does he do that others can not?

3. Stands for Something—What does he believe in? What does he do to protect what he believes in?

4. Influences Others—How does the way he lives influence or affect other people?

The Once and Future King
Name_____
Lesson 1
Date_____
Handout 2 (page 2)

Part 2

Directions: Demonstrate how these same essential elements can also be found in one other hero.

1. Mysterious Origins—

2. Superhuman Deeds—

3. Stands for Something—

4. Influences Others—

Geography and History of Britain

Directions: Review the following material.

Times

5000 B.C.–1000 B.C.—Neolithic Period

2800 B.C.–1100 B.C.—Stonehenge

1000 B.C.–55 B.C.—Celts

55 B.C.–407 A.D.—Romans

407 A.D.–449A.D.—Period of Historical Arthur

449 A.D.–1066 A.D.—Anglo-Saxon Period

1066 A.D.—Norman Invasion

Places

England

Scotland

Wales

Cornwall

Ireland

Brittany

France

Hadrian's Wall

Stonehenge

London

English Channel

Orkney Islands

Hastings

Winchester

Tintagel

Sherwood Forest

Carlisle

Caerlion

Cadbury-Camelot

Glastonbury

A Legend Develops

Directions: Note the changes and developments of the Arthurian legend.

600—Wales—poem by an unknown author, "The Goddoddin"—Arthur is portrayed as a fierce warrior.

800—Wales—Nennius "This History of the Britons"—Arthur is the leader of British armies against the Saxon invaders; wins twelve battles; Medraut and Arthur are killed at Camlann.

1019—Brittany—"The Legend of St. Goeznovius"—Arthur, the king of the Britons, leads an army to fight the Romans.

1125—England—William of Malmesbury, *"Gesta Regnum Anglorum"*—Arthur fought against the Saxons; his tomb is unknown; has many stories told about him.

1137—England—Geoffrey of Monmouth, *The History of the Kings of Britain*—Merlyn, an enchanter; Uther Pendragon, Arthur's father; sword called Caliburn; marries Guenever; Bedevere and Kay; holds court at Caerleon-upon-Usk; Mordred is mentioned; River Camel sight of a battle; carried off to Avalon to be healed of his wounds.

1155—French Channel Islands—Wace, *Roman de Brut*—Round Table mentioned for the first time; hope of Arthur's return from Avalon at some future time.

1170s—France—Chretien de Troyes, various Romances—Lancelot mentioned for the first time; Camelot mentioned for the first time; The Holy Grail; Morgan La Fay as Arthur's sister.

1200s—France—Unknown author, a series of Arthurian stories known as The Vulgate Cycle—Galahad achieves the Grail and is the son of Lancelot; Merlyn is both a prophet and an enchanter, does magic and sees into the future; Mordred is Arthur's son; the final battle on Salisbury Plain; Excalibur is thrown into the Lake; Arthur is carried out to sea.

1325—Wales—Unknown author, *The Mabinogion*—Arthur becomes a "super hero" and can do things no one else can.

1469—England—Thomas Malory, *Le Morte D'Arthur*—The ideal chivalry is embodied in the knights of the Round Table; Morgan La Fay as evil and tries to kill Arthur.

1859–1885—England—Alfred, Lord Tennyson—*The Idylls of the King*—The Legend of Arthur is applied to the time it was written; used the legend to teach people how to live or not to live; moral.

1958—England—T.H. White—*The Once and Future King*—Merlyn is old and lives backward in time; Arthur tries to find a solution to war; characters age and are psychologically true.

1961—America—Lerner and Lowe's "Camelot," a musical—Comic elements are emphasized; a romantic love triangle; Camelot is the ideal spot; associations with the Kennedys.

1960s—England—Archeological excavations—search for the "truth" behind the legends; return to origins of the legends without the medieval additions.

1970s—Scotland—Mary Stewart, *The Merlin Trilogy*—Combines well-known medieval legends with the new archeological discoveries; Merlin as narrator; Arthur is war leader during the Dark Ages.

1981—England—John Boorman's film *Excalibur*—Set in the Dark Ages with medieval armor; based on Malory; emphasis on both magic and realistic bloodshed.

Lesson 2
Malory and White

Objectives

- To introduce Malory's *Le Morte D'Arthur*
- To recognize and list important aspects of Malory's work, such as vocabulary, portrayed lifestyle, and knighthood qualities
- To examine how White uses aspects of Malory's work to create comedy in "The Sword in the Stone"

Notes the the Teacher

The opening pages of "The Sword in the Stone" are challenging to students because of many references to medieval terms, concepts, and language. This lesson is designed to provide the student with an example from Malory's *Le Morte D'Arthur* which can be read apart from the novel, discussed in terms of the vocabulary and concepts of medieval values, and applied to the student's understanding of "The Sword in the Stone."

Procedure

1. Distribute **Handouts 5** and **6**. Explain that the excerpt is from Thomas Malory's *Le Morte D'Arthur* (have students refer to **Handout 4**), that it does not directly deal with Arthur but talks about one of his knights, Sir Tristam. Students can read the excerpt on their own or the teacher can read it to them. The teacher can stop at an unfamiliar word and ask for possible definitions from students based on context clues. Students should record these in part 1 of **Handout 6**.
   Suggested Responses:
   Part 1
   1. *Truage—tax*
   2. *Bain—bath*
   3. *Eme—lord*
   4. *Meseemeth—I think*
   5. *Brachet—hunting dog*
   6. *Wit—know*
   7. *Assayed—tried*
   8. *Fewter—make a spear ready for use*
   9. *Dissever—to tell apart*
   10. *Harping—to play a harp*

   When the reading is completed, students should be ready to fill in parts 2 and 3 of **Handout 6**. This can be done individually and then compared in large or small groups.

   Suggested Responses:
   Part 2
   1. *Disputes are settled by fighting.*
   2. *A knight can do both feats of strength and things of beauty.*
   3. *Revenge is important.*
   4. *Jousts are governed by rules.*
   5. *There is a strong relationship between a lord and his knight.*
   Part 3
   1. *Play a harp*
   2. *Hunt*
   3. *Hawk*
   4. *Fight*
   5. *Is intelligent*

2. Distribute **Handout 7**. Expect students to point out parallels between the Tristram story and various incidents in "The Sword in the Stone." In a large group, the students should agree on five qualities of a good knight, based on **Handout 6**. In small groups, students recall incidents from "The Sword in the Stone" which make fun of these qualities. Students fill in the second column.
   Suggested Responses:
   Hawking—with Cully, (Chapter 1 and 2)
   Hunting—the Christmas boar hunt (Chapter 16) and Pellinore and the Questing Beast
   Fighting—(Chapter 7) the joust between Grummore and Pellinore
   Harping and singing—the Christmas feast (Chapter 15)
   Intelligence—the characterizations of Grummore and Pellinore as dim-witted.

The Story of Sir Tristram
from *Le Morte D'Arthur* by Sir Thomas Malory

Directions: Read the following excerpt.

. . . And then he let ordain a gentleman that was well learned and taught, his name was Gouvernail; and then he sent young Tristram with Gouvernail into France to learn the language, and nurture, and deeds of arms. And there was Tristram more than seven years. And then when he well could speak the language, and had learned all that he might learn in that countries, then he came home to his father, King Meliodas, again.

And so Tristram learned to be an harper passing all other, that there was none such called in no country, and so in harpingand in instruments of music he applied him in his youth for to learn. And after, as he growed in might and strength, he laboured ever in hunting and in hawking—never gentleman more, that ever we heard of. And as the book saith, he began good measures of blowing of beasts of venery, and beasts of chase, and all manner of vermins, and all these terms we have yet of hawking and hunting. And therefore the book of venery, of hawking, and hunting, is called the book of Sir Tristram.

Wherefore, as meseemeth, all gentlemen that bearen old arms ought of right to honour Sir Tristram for the goodly terms that gentlemen have and use, and shall do to the day of doom, that thereby in a manner all men of worship may dissever a gentlemen from a yeoman, and from a yeoman a villain. For he that gentle is will draw him unto gentle tatches, and to follow the customs of noble gentlemen.

Thus Tristram endured in Cornwall until he was big and strong, of the age of eighteen years. And then the King Meliodas had great joy of young Tristram, and so had the queen, his wife. For ever after in her life, because Sir Tristram saved her from the fire, she did never hate him more after, but ever loved him after, and gave Tristram many great gifts; for every estate loved him, where that he went.

Then it befell that King Anguish of Ireland sent unto King Mark of Cornwall for his truage, that Cornwall had paid many winters. And all that time King Mark was behind of the truage for seven years.

And King Mark and his barons gave unto the messenger of Ireland these words and answer, that they would none pay; and bad the messenger go unto his king Anguish.

'And tell him we will pay no truage, but tell your lord, and he will always have truage of us of Cornwall, bid him send a trusty knight of his land, that will fight for his right, and we shall find another to defend our right.'

With this answer the messengers departed into Ireland. And when King Anguish understood the answer of the messengers he was wonderly wroth. And then he called unto him Sir Marhaus, the good knight, that was nobly proved, and a knight of the Round Table. And this Marhaus was brother unto the Queen of Ireland. Then the king said thus:

'Fair brother, Sir Marhaus, I pray you go into Cornwall for my sake, to do battle for our truage that of right we ought to have; and whatsoever ye spend ye shall have sufficiently more that ye shall need.'

'Sir,' said Marhaus, 'wit ye well that I shall not be loth to do battle in the right of you and your land with the best knight of the Table Round; for I know them, for the most part, what be their deeds; and for to advance my deeds and to increase my worship I will right gladly go unto this journey for our right.'

So in all haste there was made purveyance for Sir Marhaus, and he had all thing that him needed; and so he departed out of Ireland, and arrived up in Cornwall even fast by the Castle of Tintagel. And when King Mark understood that he was there arrived to fight for Ireland, then made King Mark great sorrow when he understood that the good and noble knight Sir Marhaus was come. For they knew no knight that durst have ado with him. For at that time Sir Marhaus was called one of the famousest and renowned knights of the world.

And thus Sir Marhaus abode in the sea, and every day he sent unto King Mark for to pay truage that was behind of seven year, other-else to find a knight to fight with him for the truage. This manner of message Sir Marhaus sent daily unto King Mark.

Then they of Cornwall let make cries in every place, that what knight would fight for to save the truage of Cornwall, he should be rewarded so that he should fare the better the term of his life.

Then some of the barons said to King Mark, and counselled him to send to the court of King Arthur for to seek Sir Lancelot du Lake, that was that time named for the marvelloust knight of all the world. Then there were some other barons that counselled the king not to do so, and said that it was labour in vain, because Sir Marhaus was a knight of the Round Table, 'therefore any of them will be loth to have ado with other, but if it were any knight at his own request would fight disguised and unknown.' So the king and all his barons assented that it was no boot to seek any knight of the Round Table.

This meanwhile came the language and the noise unto King Meliodas, how that Sir Marhaus abode fast by Tintagel, and how King Mark could find no manner knight to fight for him. When young Tristram heard of this he was wroth, and sore ashamed that there durst no knight in Cornwall have ado with Marhaus of Ireland.

Therewithal Tristram went unto his father, King Melodias, and asked him counsel what was best to do to recover Cornwall from truage.

'For, as meseemeth,' said Tristram, 'it were shame that Sir Marhaus the Queen's brother of Ireland, should go away unless that he were foughten withal.'

'As for that,' said King Meliodas, 'wit you well, son Tristram, that Sir Marhaus is called one of the best knights of the world, and knight of the Table Round; and therefore I know no knight in this country that is able to match with him.'

'Alas,' said Tristram, 'that I am not made knight. And if Sir Marhaus should thus depart into Ireland, God let me never have worship; and I were made knight I should match him. And sir,' said Tristram, 'I pray you give me leave to ride to King Mark; and so ye be not displeased, of King Mark will I be made knight.'

'I will well,' said King Meliodas, 'that ye be ruled as your courage will rule you.'

Then Tristram thanked his father much. And then he made him ready to ride into Cornwall.

In the meanwhile there came a messenger with letters of love from King Faramon of France's daughter unto Tristram, that were full of piteous letters, and in them were written many complaints of love; but Tristram had no joy of her letters not regard unto her. Also she sent him a little brachet that was passing fair. But when the king's daughter understood that Tristram would not love her, as the book saith, she died for sorrow. And then the same squire that brought the letter and the brachet came again unto Tristram, as after ye shall hear in the tale following.

So after this young Tristram rode unto his eme King Mark of Cornwall. And when he came there he heard say that there would no knight fight with Sir Marhaus.

Then yede Tristram unto his eme and said, 'Sir, if ye will give me the order of knighthood, I will do battle with Sir Marhaus.'

'What are ye,' said the king, 'and from whence be ye come?'

'Sir,' said Tristram, 'I come from King Meliodas that wedded your sister, and a gentleman wit ye well I am.'

King Mark beheld Tristram and saw that he was but a young man of age, but he was passingly well and made big.

'Fair sir,' said the king, 'what is your name, and where were ye born?'

'Sir,' said he again, 'my name is Tristram, and in the country of Lionesse was I born.'

'Ye say well,' said the king; 'and if ye will do this battle I shall make you knight.'

'Therefore I come to you,' said Tristram, 'and for none other cause.'

But then King Mark made him knight. And therewithal, anon as he had made him knight, he sent a messenger unto Sir Marhaus with letters that said that he had found a young knight ready for to take the battle to the uttermost.

'It may be well so,' said Sir Marhaus; 'but tell King Mark I will not fight with no knight but he be of blood royal, that is to say, other king's son, other queen's son, born of a prince or princess.'

When King Mark understood that, he sent for Sir Tristram of Lionesse and told him what was the answer of Sir Marhaus.

Then said Sir Tristram, 'Sithen that he sayeth so, let him wit that I am comen of father side and mother side of as noble blood as he is: for, sir, now shall ye know that I am King Meliodas' son, born of your own sister, Dame Elizabeth, that died in the forest in the birth of me.'

'O Jesu,' said King Mark, 'ye are welcome fair nephew to me.'

Then in all haste the king horsed Sir Tristram, and armed him in the best matter that might be had or gotten for gold or silver. And then King Mark sent unto Sir Marhaus, and did him wit that a better born man than he himself should fight with him, 'and his name is Sir Tristram de Lionesse, begotten of King Meliodas, and born of King Mark's sister.' Then was Sir Marhaus glad and blithe that he should fight with such a gentleman.

And so by the assent of King Mark and of Sir Marhaus they let ordain that they should fight within an island nigh Sir Marhaus' ships; and so was Tristram put into a vessel both his horse and he, and all that to him longed both for his body and his horse, that he lacked nothing. And when King Mark and his barons of Cornwall beheld how young Sir Tristram departed with such a carriage to fight for the right of Cornwall, there was neither man ne woman of worship but they wept to see and understand so young a knight to jeopard himself for their right.

So to shorten this tale, when Sir Tristram was arrived within the island he looked to the farther side, and there he saw at an anchor six other ships nigh to the land; and under the shadow of the ships, upon the land, there hoved the noble knight, Sir Marhaus of Ireland. Then Sir Tristram commanded his servant Gouvernail to bring his horse to the land, and dress his harness at all manner of rights.

And then Sir Marhaus advised Sir Tristram, and said thus: 'Young knight, Sir Trisram, what dost thou here? Me sore repenteth of thy courage, for wit thou well I have been assayed with many noble knights, and the best knights of this land have been assayed of my hands, and also I have matched with the best knights of the world. And therefore by my counsel return again unto thy vessel.'

'Ah, fair knight, and well-proved knight,' said Sir Tristram, 'thou shalt well wit I may not forsake thee in this quarrel, for I am for thy sake made knight. And thou shalt well wit that I am a king's son, born and gotten upon a queen; and such promise I have made at my nephew's request and mine own seeking, that I shall fight with thee unto the uttermost, and deliver Cornwall from the old truage. And also wit thou well, Sir Marhaus, that this is the greatest cause that thou couragest me to have ado with thee, for thou art called one of the most renowned knights of the world. And because of that noise and fame that thou hast thou givest me courage to have ado with thee, for never yet was I proved with good knight; and sithen I took the order of knighthood this day, I am right well pleased that I may have ado with so good a knight as thou art. And now wit thou well, Sir Marhaus, that I cast me to get worship on thy body; and if that I be not proved, I trust to God that I shall be worshipfully proven upon thy body, and to deliver the country of Cornwall from all manner of truage from Ireland for ever.'

When Sir Marhaus had heard him say what he would, he said thus again:

'Fair knight, sithen it is so that thou castest to win worship of me, I let thee wit worship may thou none lose by me if thou mayest stand me three strokes; for I let thee wit for my noble deeds, proved and seen, King Arthur made me knight of the Table Round.'

Then they began to fewter their spears, and they met so fiercely together that they smote either other down, both horse and man. But Sir Marhaus smote Sir Tristram a great wound in the side with his spear. And then they avoided their horses, and pulled out their swords, and threw their shields afore them. And then they lashed together as men that were wild and courageous. And when they had stricken together long that their arms failed, then they left their strokes, and foined at their breasts and visors; and when they saw that that might not prevail them, then they hurtled together like rams to bear either other down.

Thus they fought still together more than a half a day, and either of them were wounded passing sore, that the blood ran down freshly from them upon the ground. By then Sir Tristram waxed more fresher that Sir Marhaus, and better winded and bigger; and with a mighty stroke he smote Sir Marhaus upon the helm such a buffet that it went through his helm, and through the coif of steel, and through the brain-pan, and the sword stuck so fast in the helm and in his brain-pan that Sir Tristram pulled three times at his sword or ever he might pull it out from his head. And there Sir Marhaus fell down on his knees, the edge of Sir Tristram's sword left in his brain-pan. And suddenly Sir Marhaus rose grovelling, and threw his sword and his shield from him, and so he ran to his ships and fled his way. And Sir Tristram had ever his shield and his sword.

And when Sir Tristram saw Sir Marhaus withdraw him, he said, 'Ah sir knight of the Round Table, why withdrawest thou thee? Thou dost thyself and thy kin great shame, for I am but a young knight, or now I was never proved, and rather than I should withdraw me from thee, I had rather be hew in piece-meal.'

Sir Marhaus answered no word but yede his way sore groaning.

'Well, sir knight,' said Sir Tristram, 'I promise thee thy sword and thy shield shall be mine; and thy shield shall I wear in all places where I ride on my adventures, and in the sight of King Arthur and all the Round Table.'

So sir Marhaus and his fellowship departed into Ireland. And as soon as he came to the king, his brother, they searched his wounds. And when his head was searched a piece of Sir Tristram's sword was founden therein and might never be had out of his head for no surgeons. And so he died of Sir Tristram's sword; and that piece of the sword the queen, his sister, kept it for ever with her, for she thought to be revenged and she might.

Now turn we again unto Sir Tristram, that was sore wounded, and full sore bled that he might not within a little while stand, when he had taken cold, unnethe stir him of his limbs. And then he set him down softly upon a hill and bled fast. Then anon came Gouvernail, his man, with his vessel; and the king and his barons came with procession against Sir Tristram.

And when he was come unto the land, King Mark took him in his arms, and the king and Sir Dinas, the Seneschal, led Sir Tristram into the Castel of Tintagel. And then he was searched in the best manner, and laid on his bed. And when King Mark saw his wounds he wept heartily and so did all his lords.

'So God me help,' said King Mark, 'I would not for all my lands that my nephew died.'

So Sir Tristram lay there a month and more, and ever he was like to die of that stroke that Sir Marhaus smote him first with the spear. For, as the French book saith, the spear's head was envenomed, that Sir Tristram might not be whole. Then was King Mark and all his barons passing heavy, for they deemed none other but that Sir Tristram should not recover. Then the king let send after all manner of leeches and surgeons, both unto men and women, and there was none that would behote him the life.

Then came there a lady that was a right wise lady, and she said plainly unto King Mark, and to Sir Tristram, and to all his barons, that he should never be whole but if Sir Tristram went into the dame country that the venom came from, and in that country should he be holpen of else never. Thus said the lady unto the king. When King Mark understood that, he let purvey for Sir Tristram a fair vessel, well victualled, and therein was put Sir Tristram, and Gouvernail with him, and Sir Tristram took his harp with him. And so he was put into the sea to sail into Ireland.

And so by good fortune he arrived up in Ireland, even fast by a castle where the king and the queen was; and at his arrival he sat and harped in his bed a merry lay, such one heard they never none in Ireland before that time. And when it was told the king and the queen of such a knight that was such an harper, anon the king sent for him, and let search his wounds, and then asked him his name.

Then he answered, 'I am of the country of Lionesse, and my name is Tramtrist, that thus was wounded in a battle as I fought for a lady's right.'

'So God me help,' said the King Anguish, 'ye shall have all the help in this land that ye may have here. But I let you wit, in Cornwall I had a great loss as ever had a king, for there I lost the best knight of the world; his name was Marhaus, a full and noble knight, and knight of the Table Round;' and there he told Sir Tristram wherefore Sir Marhaus was slain. Sir Tristram made semblant as he had been sorry, and better knew he how it was than the king.

Then the king for great favour made Tramtrist to be put in his daughter's ward and keeping, because she was a noble surgeon. And when she had searched him she found in the bottom of his wound that therein was poison, and so she healed him in a while; and therefore Tramtrist cast great love to La Beale Isoud, for she was at that time the fairest maid and lady of the world. And there Tramtrist learned her to harp, and she began to have a great fantasy unto him.

Thus was sir Tramtrist long there well cherished with the king and with the queen, and namely with La Beale Isoud.

So upon a day the queen and La Beale Isoud made a basin for Sir Tramtrist. And when he was in his bain the queen and Isoud, her daughter, roamed up and down in the chamber, whiles Gouvernail and Hebes attended upon Tramtrist. And the queen beheld his sword there as it lay upon his bed. And then by unhap the queen drew out his sword and beheld it a long while, and both they thought it a passing fair sword; but within a foot and an half of the point there was a great piece thereof broken of the edge. And when the queen espied that gap in the sword, she remembered her of a piece of a sword that was found in the brain-pan of Sir Marhaus, the good knight that was her brother.

'Alas then,' said she unto her daughter, La Beale Isoud, 'this is the same traitor knight that slew my brother, thine eme.'[1]

---

[1] Thomas Malory, *The Tales of King Arthur*, ed. Michael Senior (New York: Schocken Books, 1980), 95–103.

Name_____

Date_____

The Story of Sir Tristram by Malory

Directions: Complete the following.

Part 1

List ten words that Malory uses that are no longer in use. Guess at meanings by the way the words are used in the passage.

1.   6.

2.   7.

3.   8.

4.   9.

5.   10.

Part 2. Life in the Middle Ages

List five things that you found in this excerpt about life in the Middle Ages.

1.

2.

3.

4.

5.

Part 3. Knighthood

List five things that Sir Tristram can do or does which show that he is an exemplary knight.

1.

2.

3.

4.

5.

Name_____
Date_____

A Bit of Comedy

Directions: List some parallels between the Tristram story and various incidents in "The Sword in the Stone."

The qualities of a good knight according to Thomas Malory:	T.H. White makes fun of the quality through the following incident:

Lesson 3
To Teach a King

Objectives
- To show Merlyn's methods of teaching Arthur
- To understand the lessons Arthur learns

Notes to the Teacher
The main purpose of Book One of *The Once and Future King* is to show how Arthur is taught by Merlyn to think. These lessons which Arthur learns in "The Sword in the Stone" are the central ideas that are developed and embellished throughout the rest of the book. This lesson highlights how and what Merlyn teaches Wart in order to prepare him to be king.

Procedure
1. Have students list on the chalkboard ten characteristics of a good and bad teacher. This exercise should be given a time limit (about fifteen minutes). Explain that the list of qualities of a good teacher should be as long as the qualities of a bad teacher.

2. Distribute **Handout 8**. In a large group, students list various characterizations of Merlyn found in chapters 3, 4, and 5 of "The Sword in the Stone."
   Suggested Responses:
   Physical
   1. *White beard and mustache*
   2. *Bird droppings on shoulder*
   3. *Gown*
   4. *Glasses*
   5. *Resigned expression*

   Description of house
   1. *Stuffed animals*
   2. *Live animals*
   3. *Junk*
   4. *Books*
   5. *Stuffed birds*

   What Merlyn says
   1. *Lives backward in time*
   2. *Owl is wise*
   3. *Knows he will tutor Arthur*

   What Merlyn does
   1. *Uses magic*
   2. *Time/space travel*
   3. *Knits*
   4. *Controls weather, etc.*

Students should evaluate each characteristic as a positive or negative reason why that quality would make Merlyn a good or bad teacher for Wart.

3. Distribute **Handout 9**. In a large group, students fill in the chart, discussing what Arthur learns from each of his transformations.
   Suggested Responses:
   1. *A fish—Might as Right*
   2. *A merlin—to think*
   3. *An ant—life in a totalitarian society*
   4. *An owl—don't kill for pleasure*
   5. *A wild goose—don't fight each other and no boundaries*
   6. *A badger—man is undeveloped potential*

4. Distribute **Handout 10**. Based on the reading of chapters 9–11, students map out Arthur's forest adventure. This should be an individual project. Completed maps could be hung on the bulletin board.

5. Distribute **Handout 11**. In a large group, the two parables and the lessons drawn from them can be discussed.
   Suggested Responses:
   1. *Parable One—Don't judge by appearances; there is a reason for whatever happens.*
   2. *Parable Two—Humans are superior to animals in potential but can learn from them.*

   Encourage students to write a parable of their own and state the lesson it is intended to teach. They can try out their parables on each other to see if that lesson is communicated.

6. Distribute **Handout 12** to be used as a review and summary of Merlyn's methods and lessons. Number 1 synthesizes **Handout 9**; number 2, **Handout 10**; number 3, **Handout 11**; number 4, **Handout 7**; number 5, their reading.
   Suggested Responses, Numbers 4 and 5:
   The romantic views of a knight are not always true. He can cheat, armor rusts, etc.

   Think for yourself; don't rely on teachers, etc.

Merlyn: Arthur's Teacher

Directions: List the various characteristics of Merlyn.

	Positive or Negative?
Physical description	
1.	1.
2.	2.
3.	3.
4.	4.
5.	5.
Description of house	
1.	1.
2.	2.
3.	3.
4.	4.
5.	5.
What Merlyn says	
1.	1.
2.	2.
3.	3.
4.	4.
5.	5.
What Merlyn does	
1.	1.
2.	2.
3.	3.
4.	4.
5.	5.

Name_____

Date_____

"Education is experience and the essence of experience is self-reliance."

Directions: Fill in the chart listing what Arthur learns from each transformation.

Arthur's experience of being	What the experience teaches Arthur about self-reliance, Might and Right
1. A fish (chapter 5)	
2. A merlin (chapter 8)	
3. An ant (chapter 13)	
4. An owl (chapter 18)	
5. A wild goose (chapters 18–19)	
6. A badger (chapter 21)	

Name_____

Date_____

The Forest Adventure
(Chapters 9–11)

Directions: Draw a map showing the various stages of the Forest Adventure of Arthur and Kay. Indicate the following: the place where they enter the Forest Sauvage, where they meet Little John, Robin, and Marian; Robin's camp; their travels to Castle Chariot, Castle Chariot itself; their escape from the Griffin; and their return home. The Castle of the Forest Sauvage is indicated at the bottom of the sheet. Begin and end there.

CASTLE OF
FOREST SAUVAGE

Parables

Directions: A parable is a story which teaches a lesson. White has Merlyn and the badger both tell Arthur a parable in order to teach him a lesson. Discuss the following.

1. Merlyn tells Arthur the story about Rabbi Jachanan in chapter 9. Summarize the parable.

   What lesson does the parable teach?

2. The badger tells Arthur the Parable of Man in chapter 21. Summarize the parable.

   What lesson does it teach?

3. Write a parable of your own.

   What lesson does it teach?

Name_____

Date_____

What Has Arthur Learned?

Directions: Use the following to review and summarize Merlyn's methods and lessons.

1. Through the transformations

    1.

    2.

    3.

    4.

    5.

2. Through his forest adventure

    1.

    2.

    3.

    4.

    5.

3. Through parables

    1.

    2.

    3.

    4.

    5.

4. Through his experiences with Pellinore

    1.

    2.

    3.

    4.

    5.

5. By what Merlyn tells him directly

    1.

    2.

Lesson 4
Morgause and the Orkney Brothers

Objectives
- To introduce the land, the people, and the language of Scotland
- To show how these factors shape understanding of White's characterizations of Morgause and the Orkney brothers

Notes to the Teacher

In Book Two, "The Queen of Air and Darkness," White alternates scenes of Arthur, newly crowned king of England, coming to grips with the realities of war, with scenes of his cousins, the Orkney brothers, receiving a warped version of the education that Arthur received at the hands of Merlyn. This lesson deals with the Orkney brothers and their education which sets the stage for the conflict of values later in the novel.

Procedure

1. Distribute **Handout 13**. In a large group, students identify the characteristics of Scotland and its history from **Handout 3**.
   Suggested Responses:
   Part 1
   Cold, mountainous, barren, foggy, damp, rainy

   Part 2
   Celtic origins, enemies with the English, Hadrian's Wall separates them, etc.

   Play a recorded version of Robert Burns's "To a Mouse." (Available recordings include "The Poetry of Robert Burns and Scottish Border Ballads," read by Fredreck Worlock and R.C.M. Brookes, Caedmon Records #TC 1103.) After listening to the recording, students complete part 3.
   Suggested Responses:
   Part 3
   1. *Celtic vocabulary, open vowels, rolled "r"s, musical sounding, comparison with Irish or other Celtic languages*

2. Distribute **Handout 14** to review how Morgause and the Orkney clan are related to Arthur. It is a more detailed family tree which is given at the end of this section of the novel.

3. Distribute **Handout 15**. In the large or small groups, students fill in the chart characterizing each of the Orkney brothers.

Suggested Responses:
Gawaine—fourteen, red hair, loyal to family, upset but soon forgets
Agravaine—bully, afraid of pain, loyal to mother, kills unicorn
Gaheris—follower, goes along with others, holds back Agravaine, etc.
Gareth—ten, blond, against using strength against weakness, warns Gawaine, upset over unicorn

4. Distribute **Handout 16** which uses the opposite approach from the previous handout in studying characterization. Instead of abstracting character traits from incidents, students are asked to recall incidents which illustrate various character traits. This can be done in large or small groups for parts 1 and 2. Students then individually summarize the character of Morgause in part 3.
   Suggested Responses:
   Part 1
   1. *her lovers*
   2. *the mirror*
   3. *King Pellinore and the unicorn*
   4. *boiling the cat*

   Part 2
   1. *makes her husband go to war*
   2. *unicorn incident, Gareth bringing heather*
   3. *entertaining the king and knights*
   4. *boiling the cat*

5. Distribute **Handout 17**. Students can fill in the first column by reviewing **Handout 12**. They then find parallels in the education of the Orkney brothers.
   Suggested Responses:
   1. *St. Toirdealbhach, Mother Morlan*
   2. *Stories of revenge, superstition*
   3. *Killing to please another or for revenge, superstition, etc.*
   4. *Cruel, scheme rather than think, followers rather than leaders, etc.*

Optional Activities

1. Distribute **Handouts 18** and **19**. These handouts will help students understand the Orkney brothers' version of the birth of Arthur, found in chapter 1 of Book Two. **Handout 18** is Malory's version of the birth of Arthur, students read this and then go back to the version in the novel. On the chart in **Handout 19** they should sort out which parts of

their version come from Malory, which are children's language, and what is told in Scots dialect. This exercise shows how White manipulates Malory to aid in his characterizations.

2. Distribute **Handout 20**, a continuation of the discussion of comedy from **Handout 7**. Advise students that the comedy begun in Book One is continued in this part through the incidents listed on this handout but that the comedy in this book is used to build up the tension created by the more serious sections. This should prepare them for the lack of comedy in Book Three.

   Suggested Responses:
   1. *Irish stereotypes—drunk, superstitious, lots of blarney, mostly chapter 5*
   2. *Physical comedy—Piggy is not the typical lady for a knight, chapter 7*
   3. *Physical comedy—almost a Marx Brothers routine, chapter 9*

Name_____
Date_____

Scotland: The Land, the People, and the Language

Directions: Identify the characteristics of Scotland.

Part 1

Look at the map in **Handout 3**. By looking at the map of Scotland and the Orkney Islands, make some observations about the geography, climate, and living conditions that you would expect to find in Scotland.

Part 2

From what you learned about the history of the British Isles in **Handout 3**, make some observations about the people of Scotland: their origins, attitudes toward England, language, the effect of Hadrian's Wall, etc.

Part 3

The following is a poem by Robert Burns, one of Scotland's most famous poets. Read it on your own. Then listen to it read by a Scotsman. Make some observations about the language. Does it remind you of any other language? How does it differ from standard English? How do you account for these dialect differences?

To a Mouse
**ON TURNING HER UP IN HER NEST WITH
THE PLOW, NOVEMBER, 1785**[1]

Wee, sleekit°, cow'rin', tim'rous beastie,	*sleek*
O, what a panic's in thy breastie!	
Thou need na start awa sae hasty,	
Wi' bickering brattle![2]	
I wad be laith° to rin an' chase thee	*loath*
Wi'murd'ring pattle!°	*plowstaff*
I'm truly sorry man's dominion	
Has broken Nature's social union,	
An' justifies that ill opinion	
Which makes thee startle	
At me, thy poor, earth-born companion,	
An' fellow mortal!	
I doubt na, whiles,° but thou may thieve:	*sometimes*
What then? poor beastie, thou maun° live!	*must*
A daimen-icker in a thrave[3]	
'S a sma' request:	
I'll get a blessin' wi' the lave,°	*remainder*
And never miss't!	
Thy wee-bit housie, too, in ruin!	
Its silly° wa's the win's are strewin'!	*feeble*
An' naething, now, to big° a new ane,	*build*
O' foggage° green!	*moss*
An' bleak December's winds ensuin',	
Baith snell° an' keen!	*bitter*
Thou saw the fields laid bare and waste,	
An' weary winter comin' fast	
An' cozie here, beneath the blast,	
Thou thought to dwell,	
Till crash! the cruel coulter° passed	*cutter-blade*
Out-through thy cell.	
That wee-bit heap o' leaves an' stibble°	*stubble*
Has cost thee mony a weary nibble!	
Now thou's turned out, for a' thy trouble,	
But° house or hald,[4]	*without*
To thole° the winter's sleety dribble,	*endure*
An' cranreuch° cauld!	*hoarfrost*

[1]Burns's brother said that this poem was composed on the occasion it describes.
[2]With headlong scamper.
[3]An occasional ear in 24 sheaves.
[4]Hold, holding (i.e., land).

But Mousie, thou art no thy lane,[5]
In proving foresight may be vain:
The best-laid schemes o' mice an' men
    Gang aft a-gley,[6]
An' lea'e us nought but grief an' pain,
    For promised joy.

Still thou art blest compared wi'me!
The present only toucheth thee:
But och! I backward cast my e'e
    On prospects drear!
An' forward though I canna see,
    I guess an' fear![1]
1785[1]

[5]Not alone.
[6]Go oft awry.

[1]Robert Burns, "To a Mouse" in *The Norton Anthology of English Literature*, Vol. II (New York: W.W. Norton and Co., Inc., 1968), 26–27.

Arthur's Family Tree

Directions: Review how Morgause and the Orkney clan are related.

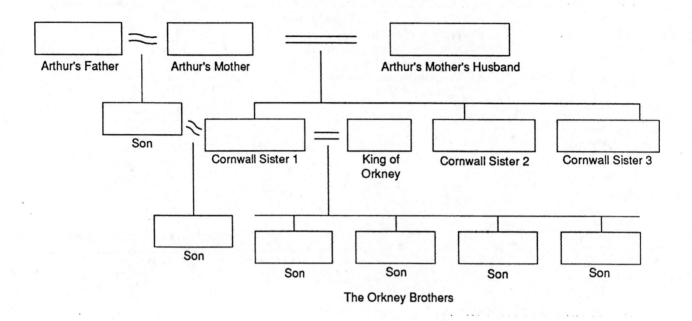

The Once and Future King
Lesson 4
Handout 15

The Orkney Brothers

Directions: Complete the following chart.

	Gawaine	Agravaine	Gaheris	Gareth
Age/Physical description (ch. 1)				
Ideas on the feud with the English (ch.1)				
Part in the killing of the unicorn (ch.7)				
Part in the fight (ch. 9)				
Reactions to Arthur's court (ch. 14)				
Attitude toward Morgause (throughout)				

Name_____
Date_____

Morgause: The Queen of Air and Darkness

Directions: Recall incidents which illustrate the various character traits.

Part 1

Show how these adjectives can be applied to Morgause by giving examples of what she does in Book Two.

1. beautiful

2. vain

3. scheming

4. cruel

Part 2

Evaluate Morgause by stating incidents from Book Two which show her in the following roles.

1. a wife

2. a mother

3. a queen

4. a sorceress

Part 3

In a brief paragraph summarize the character of Morgause. Include all of the above information.

Name_____
Date_____

Arthur and the Orkneys:
Differences in Education

Directions: Complete the chart by finding parallels between the characters listed.

Arthur	The Orkney Brothers
1. Teacher(s)	1. Teacher(s)
2. The ways he was taught	2. The ways they were taught
3. The lessons learned	3. The lessons learned
4. The effect on the person	4. The effect on the brothers

The Birth of Arthur

Directions: Read Malory's version of Arthur's birth before comparing it to White's version.

It befell in the days of Uther Pendragon, when he was king of all England, and so reigned, that there was a mighty duke in Cornwall that held war against him long time. And the duke was called the Duke of Tintagel. And so by means King Uther sent for this duke, charging him to bring his wife with him, for she was called a fair lady, and a passing wise, and her name was called Igraine.

So when the duke and his wife were comen unto the king, by the means of great lords they were accorded both. The king liked and loved this lady well, and he made them great cheer out of measure, and desired to have lain by her. But she was a passing good woman, and would not assent unto the king.

And then she told her husband, and said, 'I suppose that we were sent for that I should be dishonored. Wherefore, husband, I counsel you that we depart from hence suddenly, that we may ride all night unto our own castle.'

And in like wise as she said so they departed, that neither the king nor none of his council were ware of their departing.

All so soon as King Uther knew of their departing so suddenly, he was wonderly wroth. Then he called to him his privy council, and told them of the sudden departing of the duke and his wife. Then they advised the king to send for the duke and his wife by a great charge:

'And if he will not come at your summons, then may ye do your best, then have ye cause to make mighty war upon him.'

So that was done, and the messengers had their answers, and that was this shortly, that neither he not his wife would not come at him. Then was the king wonderly wroth. And then the king sent him plain word again, and bad him be ready and stuff him and garnish him, for within forty days he would fetch him out of the biggest castle that he hath.

When the duke had this warning, anon he went and furnished and garnished two strong castles of his, of the which the one hight Tintagel, and the other castle hight Terrabil. So his wife Dame Igraine he put in the Castle of Tintagel, and himself he put in the Castle of Terrabil, the which had many issues and posterns out. Then in all haste came Uther with a great host, and laid a siege about the Castle of Terrabil, and there he pitched many pavilions, and there was great war made on both parties, and much people slain.

Then for pure anger and for great love of fair Igraine the King Uther fell sick. So came to the King Uther Sir Ulfius, a noble knight, and asked the king why he was sick.

'I shall tell thee,' said the king. 'I am sick for anger and for love of fair Igraine that I may not be whole.'

'Well, my lord,' said Sir Ulfius, 'I shall seek Merlin, and he shall do you remedy, that your heart shall be pleased.'

So Ulfius departed, and by adventure he met Merlin in a beggar's array, and there Merlin asked Ulfius whom he sought. And he said he had little ado to tell him.

'Well,' said Merlin, 'I know whom thou seekest, for thou seekest Merlin; therefore seek no farther, for I am he, and if King Uther will well reward me, and be sworn unto me to fulfil my desire, that shall be his honour and profit more than mine, for I shall cause him to have all his desire.'

'All this I will undertake,' said Ulfius, 'than there shall be nothing reasonable but thou shalt have thy desire.'

'Well,' said Merlin,'he shall have his intent and desire. And therefore,' said Merlin, 'ride on your way, for I will not be long behind.'

Then Ulfius was glad, and rode on more than in a pace till that he came to King Uther Pendragon, and told him he had met with Merlin.

'Where is he?' said the king.

'Sir,' said Ulfius, 'he will not dwell long.'

Therewithal Ulfius was ware where Merlin stood at the porch of the pavillion's door. And then Merlin was bound to come to the king. When King Uther saw him, he said he was welcome.

'Sir,' said Merlin, 'I know all your heart every deal. So ye will be sworn unto me as ye be a true king anointed, to fulfil my desire, ye shall have your desire.'

Then the king was sworn upon the four Evangelists.

'Sir,' said Merlin, 'this is my desire: the first night that ye shall lie by Igraine ye shall get a child on her; and when that is born, that it shall be delivered to me for to nourish thereas I will have it; for it shall be your worship, and the child's avail as mickle as the child is worth.'

'I will well,' said the king, 'as thou wilt have it.'

'Now make you ready,' said Merlin, 'this night ye shall lie with Igraine in the Castle of Tintagel. And ye shall be like the duke her husband, Ulfius shall be like Sir Brastias, a knight of the duke's. But wait ye make not many questions with her nor her men, but say ye are diseased, and so hie you to bed, and rise nor on the morn till I come to you, for the Castle of Tintagel is but ten miles hence.'

So this was done as they desired. But the Duke of Tintagel espied how the king rode from the siege of Terrabil, and therefore that night he issued out of the castle at a postern for to have distressed the king's host. And so, through his own issue, the duke himself was slain or-ever the king came at the Castle of Tintagel.

So after the death of the duke, King Uther lay with Igraine more than three hours after his death and begat on her that night Arthur; and, or day came, Merlin came to the king, and bad him make ready, and so he kissed the lady Igraine and departed in all haste. But when the lady heard tell of the duke her husband, and by all record he was dead or-ever King Uther came to her, then she marvelled who that might be that lay with her in likeness of her lord. So she mourned privily and held her peace.

Then all the barons by one assent prayed the king of accord betwixt the lady Igraine and him. The king gave them leave, for fain would he have been accorded with her. So the king put all the trust in Ulfius to entreat between them. So by the entreaty at the last the king and she met together.

'Now will we do well,' said Ulfius. 'Our king is a lusty knight and wifeless, and my lady Igraine is a passing fair lady; it were great joy unto us all, and it might please the king to make her his queen.'

Unto that they all well accorded and moved it to the king. And anon, like a lusty knight, he assented thereto with good will, and so in all haste they were married in a morning with great mirth and joy.

And King Lot of Lothian and of Orkney then wedded Margawse that was Gawain's mother, and King Nentres of the land of Garlot wedded Elaine. All this was done at the request of King Uther. And the third sister Morgan le Fay was put to school in a nunnery, and there she learned so much that she was a great clerk of necromancy. And after she was wedded to King Uriens of the land of Gore, that was Sir Uwain's le Blanchemains father.

Then Queen Igraine waxed daily greater and greater. So it befell after within half a year, as King Uther lay by his queen, he asked her, by the faith she ought to him, whose was the child within her body; then [was] she sore abashed to give answer.

'Dismay you not,' said the king, 'but tell me the truth, and I shall love you the better, by the faith of my body.'

'Sir,' said she, 'I shall tell you the truth. The same night that my lord was dead, the hour of his death, as his knights record, there came into my castle of Tintagel a man like my lord in speech and in countenance, and two knights with him in likeness of his two knights Brastias and Jordans, and so I went unto bed with him as I ought to do with my lord, and the same night, as I shall answer unto God, this child was begotten upon me.'

'That is truth,' said the king, 'as ye say; for it was I myself that came in the likeness. And therefore dismay you not, for I am father to the child; and there he told her all the cause, how it was by Merlin 's counsel. Then the queen made great joy when she knew who was the father of her child.

Soon came Merlin unto the king, and said, 'Sir, ye must purvey you for the nourishing of your child.'

'As thou wilt,' said the king, 'be it.'

'Well,' said Merlin, 'I know a lord of yours in this land, that is a passing true man and a faithful, and he shall have the nourishing of your child; and his name is Sir Ector, and he is a lord of fair livelihood in many parts in England and Wales. And this lord, Sir Ector, let him be sent for, for to come and speak with you, and desire him yourself, as he loveth you, that he will put his own child to nourishing to another woman, and that his wife nourish yours. And when the child is born let it be delivered to me at yonder privy postern unchristened.'

So like as Merlin devised it was done. And when Sir Ector was come he made fiance to the king for to nourish the child like as the king desired; and there the king granted Sir Ector great rewards. Then when the lady was delivered, the king commanded two knights and two ladies to take the child, bound in cloth of gold, 'and that ye deliver him to what poor man ye meet at the postern gate of the castle.' So the child was delivered unto Merlin, and so he bare it forth unto Sir Ector, and made an holy man to christen him, and named him Arthur. And so Sir Ector's wife nourished him with her own pap.

Then within two years King Uther fell sick of a great malady. And in the meanwhile his enemies usurped upon him, and did a great battle upon his men, and slew many of his people.

'Sir,' said Merlin, 'ye may not lie so as ye do, for ye must to the field though ye ride on an horse-litter; for ye shall never have the better of your enemies but if your person be there, and then ye shall have the victory.'

So it was done as Merlin had devised, and they carried the king forth in an horse-litter with a great host toward his enemies. And at St. Albans there met with the king a great host of the north. And that day Sir Ulfius and Sir Brastias did great deeds of arms, and King Uther's men overcame the northern battle and slew many people, and put the remnant to flight. And then the king returned to London, and made great joy on his victory.

And then he fell passing sore sick, so that three days and three nights he was speechless; wherefore all the barons made great sorrow, and asked Merlin what counsel were best.

'There is none other remedy,' said Merlin, 'but God will have his will. But look ye all, barons, be before King Uther to-morn, and God and I shall make him to speak.'

So on the morn all the barons with Merlin came tofore the king; then Merlin said aloud unto King Uther,

'Sire, shall your son Arthur be king, after your days, of this realm with all the appurtenance?'

Then Uther Pendragon turned him, and said in hearing of them all.

'I give him God's blessing and mine, and bid him pray for my soul, and righteously and worshipfully that he claim the crown upon forfeiture of my blessing.' And therewith he yielded up the ghost. And then was he interred as longed to a king, wherefore the queen, fair Igraine, made great sorrow, and all the barons.[1]

[1]Malory, *Tales of King Arthur*, 29–33.

The Story of Arthur's Birth:
The Orkney Brothers' Version

Directions: Sort out the various components of Arthur's birth.

Malory Language	Children's Language	Scots Dialect

Comedy Tonight

Directions: In your own words explain how White creates comedy through the following:

1. Mother Morlan and St. Toirdealbhach

2. The romance of Pellinore and Piggy

3. Palomidies, Grummore, and the Questing Beast

Lesson 5
War and the Ideal

Objectives
- To enable student discovery of T.H. White's views on formulation of their own views
- To trace the development of Arthur's ideal of "Might for Right" and the way he puts it into practice

Notes to the Teacher
This lesson deals with the second major theme of Book Two: the development of Arthur's ideal of "Might for Right." It is a continuation of Merlyn's teaching of Arthur from Book One.

Procedure
1. Distribute **Handout 21**. In large group discussion, students answer the questions based on their reading or by looking at the text, especially chapters 2, 3, and 4.
   Suggested Responses:
   1. Gaelic War
   2. English/Celtic reasons
   3. Morgause and revenge
   4. exuberant
   5. war leads to division
   6. disintegration
   7. self-defense
   8. passive aggression
   9. aggression
   10. reason can tell

2. Distribute **Handout 22**. In small groups, students discuss their own views on the reasons for and against engaging in a war. A secretary should record viewpoints on the handout. Groups share their conclusions with the class.

3. Distribute **Handout 23**. Students follow Arthur's logic which enables him to go from an individual's warlike nature to the Round Table.
   Suggested Responses:
   Might must work for Right; Might can be used for good; make it fashionable; turn a bad thing into good; no jealousy

Optional Activity
Distribute **Handout 24**. In large or small groups, based on reading of chapter 12, students list the traditional way of fighting a battle and the way Arthur fights the Battle of Bedegraine.

Suggested Responses:
Traditional—formal, poor soldiers do all the real fighting, knights in no real danger
Arthur's way—attack at night, surprise, attack the knights

43

War (Merlyn's View)

Directions: Answer the following questions which are based on your reading.

1. With whom is Arthur engaged in war?

2. According to Merlyn, what are the racial reasons for this war?

3. According to Merlyn, what are the personal reasons for this war?

4. What is Arthur's reaction to this war?

5. According to Merlyn, why is this attitude wrong?

6. According to Merlyn, what are the usual results of a war?

7. According to Merlyn, what is the only reason for waging war?

8. What are some of Arthur's objections to this view?

9. What are some of Kay's objections to this view?

10. What are Merlyn's responses to these objections?

War (Your Views)

Directions: Complete the chart in preparation for discussion.

Reasons for engaging in a war	Reasons for not engaging in a war

The Ideal
(Chapters 6 and 8)

Direction: Examine Arthur's logic in the following exercise.

1. The Round Table _____

2. _____

3. _____

4. _____

5. _____

6. _____

7. The Round Table _____

The Once and Future King
Lesson 5
Handout 24

Name_____
Date_____

The Battle of Bedegraine

Directions: Arthur wins the Battle of Bedegraine because he breaks all established rules of battle. List those rules in the left column and Arthur's way of battle in the right column.

The Establshed Rules (What Lot expects Arthur to do)	What Arthur Does

Lesson 6
Lancelot: The Making of a Knight

Objectives

- To trace the development of Lancelot as a knight of the Round Table
- To compare Lancelot's development with Arthur's and the Orkney brothers'

Notes to the Teacher

In Book Three of *The Once and Future King*, T. H. White moves away from the comedy of Books One and Two to a more tragic view. With the introduction of Lancelot in "The Ill-Made Knight," White begins to chronicle the events which will lead to the ultimate destruction of Arthur's ideal. This lesson focuses on White's portrayal of the character of Lancelot. It is unconventional and should surprise students who have seen *Camelot*. This Lancelot is not the dashing, handsome, romantic knight that most imagine. He is, rather, an ugly tortured soul who discovers a wide gap between his idealism and reality.

Procedure

1. Distribute **Handout 25** which covers the first six chapters of "The Ill-Made Knight." In a large group, students answer these questions. Students could also prepare the answers to these questions ahead of time and share them with the class.

2. Distribute **Handout 26**. Play a recording of the song from *Camelot*, "C'est Moi" sung by Lancelot (Original Broadway Cast Recording—Columbia Records #S32602). Have students make a list of similarities (*gives his all to Arthur's ideal, great physical feats, spiritual feats, works a miracle, etc.*) and differences (*more conceited, handsome, etc.*).

3. Distribute **Handout 27**. Explain that just as Merlyn taught Arthur through the adventure of the Forest Sauvage, Lancelot is taught some important lessons through his many quests detailed in chapters 7 and 8. We also learn things about Lancelot through his reactions to these adventures. Students fill in column two of the handout by referring to the chapters.
Suggested Responses:
Arthur's ideal not shared by everyone, family considerations vs. the ideal; his own helplessness, his attractiveness to women, using Might for Right, etc.

4. Distribute **Handout 28**. Refer students to chapter 16 where White mentions the Eternal Triangle with Arthur and Guenever, but also in various relationships involving Arthur, Guenever, Elaine, and God. Use the diagram to sort out these various relationships.
Suggested Responses:
Lancelot wants to do miracles, God expects him to be pure; Elaine wants Lancelot's love, Lancelot wants not to hurt Elaine; Lancelot wants Arthur's love, at the same time wants Guenever; Arthur is his king but Lancelot wants Guenever; Guenever wants honesty but wants Lancelot to be the best knight, etc.

Hopefully, this exercise will show students how Lancelot gets caught in the middle and is pulled in opposite directions by all of these persons.

Optional Activity

Have students complete **Handout 29** individually. Hang completed sheets on the bulletin board.

Lancelot: The Making of a Knight of the Round Table

Directions: Complete the following.

1. Describe Lancelot physically.

2. Why is this description unexpected?

3. What is the name Lancelot gives himself, and what does it mean?

4. Chapter 2 begins with White's comparing Lancelot to Bradman and Wooley, two famous Cricket players from England:

   1. What qualities of Bradman and Wooley does White apply to Lancelot?

   2. To what contemporary American sports figures could you compare Lancelot in order to highlight those same qualities?

5. What are Lancelot's attitudes and emotions concerning Arthur and his ideal?

6. What specifically does Lancelot hope to gain by being Arthur's "best knight"?

7. What are some of the components of Lancelot's training?

8. Compare Uncle Dap as Lancelot's teacher to the other two teachers: Merlyn and St. Toirdealbhach.

9. In addition to physical training, what else does Lancelot consider to be an important part of being the "best knight"?

10. Why is Lancelot jealous of
    1. Guenever?

    2. Gawaine?

11. Describe Guenever physically.

12. Why is this description unexpected?

13. How does Lancelot think of Guenever at first?

    How and why does he change his impression?

14. Contrast the viewpoints of Arthur and Uncle Dap when they realize that Lancelot and Guenever are in love with each other.

15. Why is his "Word" important to Lancelot?

16. "If Lancelot were not so jealous of his Word, the tragedy would not have happened." Based on what you have read so far, explain this statement.

"C'est Moi"

Directions: The following are the lyrics to the song from the musical *Camelot* which introduces the character of Lancelot. Read them and list the similarities and the differences in the characterizations of Lancelot in the song and in the opening chapters of "The Ill-Made Knight."

LANCELOT (*sings*)

Camelot! Camelot!
In far off France I heard your call.
Camelot! Camelot!
And here I am to give my all.
I know in my soul what you expect of me;
And all that and more I shall be!

A knight of the Table Round should be invincible;
Succeed where a less fantastic man would fail;
Climb a wall no one else can climb;
Cleave a dragon in record time;
Swim a moat in a coat of heavy iron mail.
No matter the pain he ought to be unwinceable,
Impossible deeds should be his daily fare.
But where in the world
Is there in the world
A man so *extraordinaire*?

C'est moi! C'est moi!
I'm forced to admit!
'Tis I, I humbly reply.
That mortal who
These marvels can do,
C'est moi! C'est moi, 'tis I.
I've never lost
In battle or game.
I'm simply the best by far.
When swords are cross'd
'Tis always the same:
One blow and *au revoir!*
C'est moi! C'est moi,
So admir'bly fit;
A French Prometheus unbound.
And here I stand with valor untold,
Exception'lly brave, amazingly bold,
To serve at the Table Round!

The soul of a knight should be a thing remarkable
His heart and his mind as pure as morning dew.
With a will and a self-restraint
That's the envy of ev'ry saint,
He could easily work a miracle of two!
To love and desire he ought to be unsparkable.
The ways of the flesh should offer no allure.
But where in the world
Is there in the world
A man so untouch'd and pure?
C'est moi!
C'est moi! C'est moi!

I blush to disclose
I'm far too noble to lie.
That man in whom
These qualities bloom,
C'est moi,
C'est moi, 'tis I!

I've never stray'd
From all I believe.
I'm bless'd with an iron will.
Had I been made
The partner of Eve,
We'd be in Eden still.
C'est moi! C'est moi,
The angels have chose
To fight their battles below.
And here I stand as pure as a pray'r,
Incredibly clean, with virtue to spare,
The godliest man I know . . .!
C'est moi![1]

Similarities	Differences

[1]Lerner and Lowe, *Camelot* (New York: Dell Laurel Leaf Library, 1967), 184–186.

Name_____
Date_____

Lancelot's Quest

Directions: Complete the following chart based on your reading.

The incident	What Lancelot learns or what we learn about Lancelot
1. Saves Gawaine from Sir Carados	
2. Meets his cousin Lionel	
3. Taken prisoner ar Castle Chariot	
4. Released by King Bagdemagus's daughter	
5. Battles the knight of the Pavillion	
6. Wins the tournament for King Bagdemagus	
7. Fights Sir Tarquine and saves the captive knights	
8. Battles the fat knight who tricks him	
9. Battles the knight who wants to behead his adulterous wife	

Name_____
Date_____

The Eternal Quadrangle
(Chapters 10–18)

Directions: Use the following diagram to sort out the various relationships.

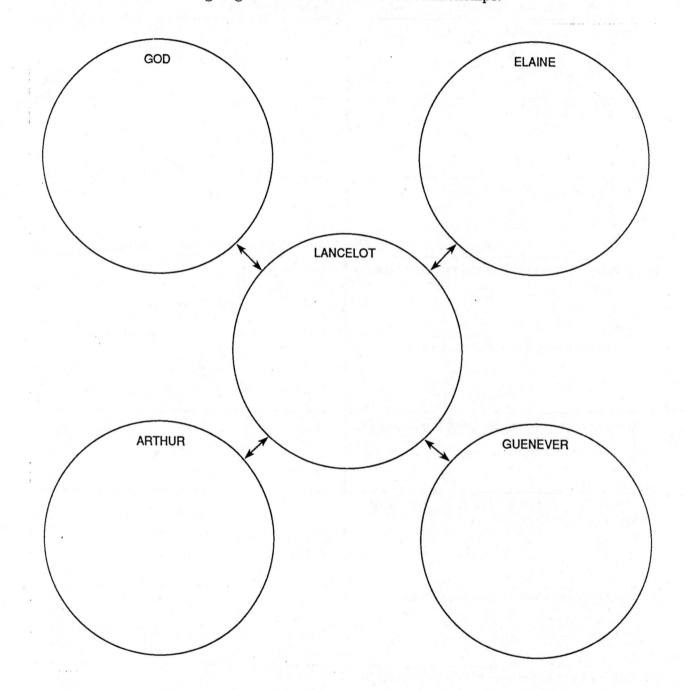

Name_____

Date_____

Heraldry

Directions: Draw the coats of arms of the following, based on the descriptions in "The Ill-Made Knight."

Terms: Or—gold or yellow; argent—silver or white; gules—red; azure—blue; sable—black; rampant—standing up on hind legs

ARTHUR

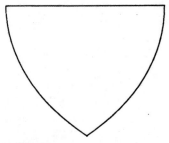

Chapter 4—

Or, a dragon rampant gules

LANCELOT

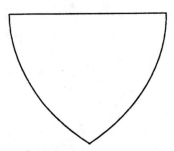

Chapter 8—

Argent, a bend gules

On the shield to the right, design a coat of arms for yourself.

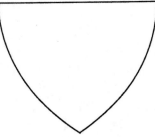

Be sure to place your name above the shield and include a description in heraldic terms below it.

LE CHEVALIER MAL FET

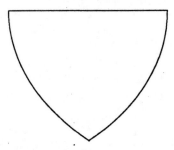

Chapter 23—

a silver crowned woman on a sable field with a knight kneeling at her feet

GALAHAD

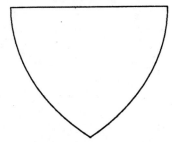

Chapter 28—

Argent, a Tau cross gules

Lesson 7
The Decline of the Ideal

Objective
- To trace the causes and signs of the decline in Arthur's ideal

Notes to the Teacher
The second half of "The Ill-Made Knight" traces the signs of decay in Arthur's ideal. Students should be aware that the end of Arthur's ideal comes about as a direct result of the strengths and weaknesses of the characters involved. The emphasis on characterization in previous lessons should prepare students for the tragedy detailed in Book Four. Things are happening because the people involved are who they are by reason of their education, environment, ideals, and choices they have made.

Procedure
1. Distribute **Handout 30** to be done individually and shared with the entire class or done as a large group activity.
   Suggested Responses:
   Part 1
   1. Knights become heroes
   2. No need for armies
   3. Travel freely
   4. Civilized manners
   5. Law courts
   6. All think as Englishmen
   7. New knights come to Camelot

   Part 2
   1. Morgause takes husband's killer as lover
   2. Gawaine killed Pellinore in revenge
   3. Agravaine kills Morgause
   4. Mordred stabs Lamorak in the back

   Part 3
   1. Arthur channeled Might for Right
   2. Now Right has triumphed over Might
   3. Set Might against the spirit to work for God
   4. Set up Quest for Holy Grail
      Other answers will vary.

2. Distribute **Handout 31**. Students can do this on their own and share with the entire class or as a large or small group activity.
   Suggested Responses:
   Part 1
   Journey to find something

Part 2
1. Cup used by Christ at Last Supper
2. Symbolizes presence of God

Part 3
1. Gawaine—misses the point
2. Bors—not to commit sin
3. Lionel—God tests his brother
4. Aglovale—end feud with Orkneys
5. Percivale—perfect innocence
6. Galahad—like and angel
7. Lancelot—recognizes his sins

Part 4
1. Ideal still in trouble
2. Best knights lost
3. Lancelot wants to break relationship with Guenever
4. Arthur sees quest as a failure

3. Distribute **Handout 32**. Follow procedures for **Handout 28**. Students should recognize that the positions are more extreme than before. (God demands purity but gives Lancelot his miracle anyway; Elaine's suicide; Arthur loves both Lancelot and Guenever; Guenever demands Lancelot love her more than God and only wins him back by surrendering her possessiveness; Lancelot loves Guenever and God equally, does not want to tell Elaine, wears Elaine's sleeve in tournament, etc.).

Arthur's Ideal Begins to Decline
(Chapters 25—27)

Directions: Complete the following.

Part 1

In what ways does Arthur's ideal seem to be fulfilled?

1.

2.

3.

4.

5.

6.

7.

Part 2

Beneath the surface, however, we can see beginnings of the declining of the ideal. The agents of this decline are the Orkney clan. What do each of the following do which undermines Arthur's ideal?

1. Morgause

2. Gawaine

3. Agravaine

4. Mordred

Part 3

Arthur must then rethink his ideal:

1. What has he done to establish Right of Justice in his kingdom?

2. What problem with Might does he now face?

3. In what ways does he plan to rechannel Might?

4. What may be the result of his rechanneling Might?

5. What question does this raise concerning the possible outcome?

6. What does Lancelot propose they do?

The Quest for the Holy Grail
(Chapters 28–33)

Directions: Complete the following.

Part 1

Define a *quest*.

Part 2

What is the reality and the symbolism of the Grail?

1. Reality

2. Symbolic meaning

Part 3

More important than finding the object which is being sought in a quest is what the seeker finds out about himself on the quest. What do each of the following knights find out about themselves or about life in general by going on the quest?

1. Gawaine

2. Bors

3. Lionel

4. Aglovale

5. Percivale

6. Galahad

7. Lancelot

Part 4

What effect did the quest have on the following?

1. Arthur's ideal

2. The Round Table

3. Lancelot and Guenever

4. Arthur himself

The Eternal Quadrangle—Again
(Chapters 37–40)

Directions: Continue to examine the various relationships.

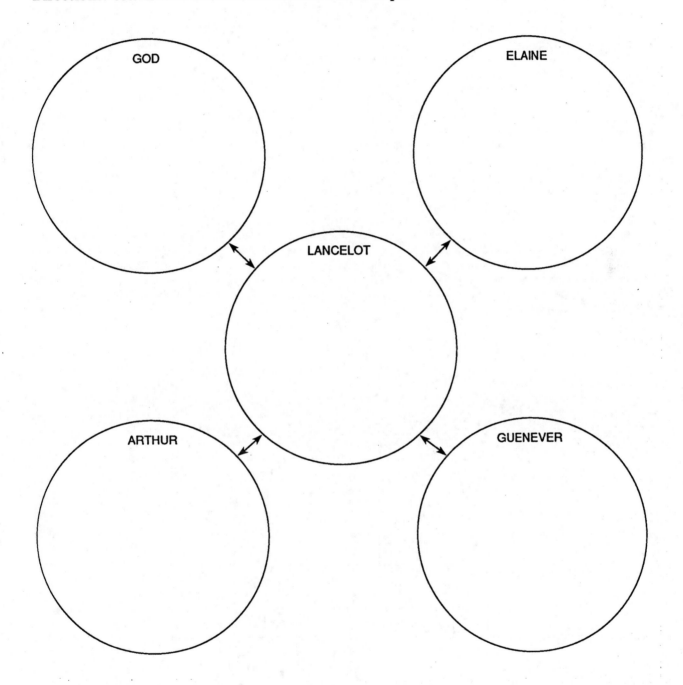

Lesson 8
The Candle in the Wind

Objectives
- To follow the destruction of Arthur's ideal
- To summarize Arthur's review of his life
- To evaluate the summary as optimistic or pessimistic

Notes to the Teacher
The final book of *The Once and Future King* tells the familiar story of the destruction of the Round Table and, with it, Arthur's ideal. Once again, White emphasizes this inevitability by reminding us that the characters who act out this drama are acting the only way they can—Arthur, still trying to improve his ideal, is trapped by it. Mordred is acting as he has been taught; Lancelot and Guenever are trapped by their love. As these events unfold, Arthur sees his world fall apart and wonders about the value of it all. Students will be asked to evaluate whether they believe White ends the novel on a positive or negative note. This lesson aims to have students use the book to support statements by citing quotes from the text.

Procedure
1. Distribute **Handout 33** to be done as an individual or small group activity to help students review past material (questions 2 and 3) and to add new material (questions 1, 4, and 5).

2. Distribute **Handout 34** to be done as a teacher-led activity. It is designed to help students find evidence in the text.

3. Distribute **Handout 35**. Number 1 is designed for using the text. Number 2 asks for a summary of the story of David and Bathsheba (2 Samuel 11), which students should research if necessary. Number 3 asks for parallels between the story and what is happening in the novel (the adultery of Lancelot and Guenever).

4. Distribute **Handout 36**, a follow-up to **Handout 34**. Students do this on their own and share results with the entire group. The teacher may lead the discussion on which is best evidence.

5. Distribute **Handout 37** (part 1), an individual or large group activity acting as a summary of the final chapter.

Suggested Responses:
1. perfectible
2. an agent of that perfection
3. decent and being potentially perfect
4. a. Right
   b. be used for Right
   c. remained
   d. Spiritual realm
      1. lost or taken away
      2. unchanged
   e. laws
   f. armies and war
5. children's illusions
6. Homo ferox; ferocious man
7. machine in a senseless universe
   a. slaughter
   b. appealing
   c. national movements
   d. wrong; slaughter
   e. repercussions later
   f. not do
   g. forget the past
   h. the right materials
   i. possession
   j. share
   k. useless
   l. fear or reliability
   m. word
8. a. the bishop
   b. fight in battle
   c. his ideal
   d. a candle in the wind
   e. let the candle go out
9. Merlyn
   a. Merlyn taught him through animals
   b. an animal
   c. looking at other species
   d. nothing
      1. imaginary
      2. culture and civilizations
      3. boundaries
10. return to the world
11. culture
12. less than a drop

6. Distribute **Handout 37** (part 2). In small groups, students evaluate the ideas in part 1 as optimistic or pessimistic. These should be shared with the entire class in a discussion of part 3 of **Handout 37**.

Name_____
Date_____

The Evolving Ideal

Directions: Complete the following based on both past and new material.

1. What things were like in Uther's Day (Book Four, chapter 3)

2. Arthur's early ideal (see previous handouts)

3. Arthur's ideal before the quest for the Grail (see **Handout 30**)

4. Arthur's ideal becomes law (Book Three, chapter 45)

5. Arthur's law is used against him (Book Four, chapter 5)

Name_____
Date_____

Mordred

Directions: Find evidence in the text to support these ideas.

1. His upbringing (end of chapter 1)

2. His part in the conspiracy to tell Arthur (chapters 1–2)

3. His reasons for telling Arthur (chapter 1)

4. His part in the fight with his brothers (chapter 2)

5. Arthur's feelings toward him (chapter 4)

6. A physical description of Mordred (Book Three, chapter 27)

The Justice Room

Directions: Complete the following.

1. Describe Arthur's Justice Room (Book Four, chapter 5).

2. Find out what is the biblical story of David and Bathsheba.

3. How is this biblical story symbolic of the action in Book Four?

Name_____

Date_____

The Decline of King Arthur

Directions: Trace the decline of King Arthur by indicating how he is described in the following chapters from "The Candle in the Wind."

1. Last paragraph of chapter 2

2. Chapter 4—after the page has announced him to Lancelot and Guenever

3. Chapter 5—after he enters the Justice Room

4. Chapter 8—as he enters the Justice Room awaiting Guenever's execution

5. Chapter 8—as he goes to the window to watch Guenever's execution

6. Chapter 10—as he enters to receive Guenever back from Lancelot

7. Chapter 10—when he is forced to condemn Lancelot

8. Chapter 11—what Guenever and Agnes say about his condition

9. Chapter 14—awaiting the battle on Salisbury Plain

The Candle in the Wind

Part 1
Directions: In this chapter Arthur reviews his life and work. Complete the following outline of this review.

1. Merlyn taught Arthur that Man was _____

2. The whole purpose of Arthur's life was to be _____

3. This purpose, however, is based on the false idea that Man is _____

4. Arthur has spent his whole life trying to "dam the flood."

   a. He tried to crush Might by using _____

   b. He tried to harness Might to _____

   c. These ends were achieved but Might_____

   d. He tried to rechannel Might to _____

      1. Those who achieved this were _____

      2. Those who did not returned _____

   e. He tried to bend Might through _____

   f. This too failed because of the rise of _____

5. Arthur comes to the conclusion that Chivalry and Justice are _____

6. He also concludes that Man is not "Homo Sapiens," thinking man, but _____

_____which means _____

7. He comes to the conclusion that Man is neither good nor evil but only a _____

   a. Wicked leaders lead their people to _____

   b. They offer something to those they lead which is _____

   c. Wars are _____

   d. Man avenges wrong with_____; slaughter with _____

   e. Any action in one gerneration has _____

   f. The only thing to do is_____for fear of causing some future harm.

g. The only way to stop war is _____

h. Man cannot do this because he cannot choose _____

i. Wars are fought over _____

j. The Church remedy is to _____

k. To Arthur this is _____

l. War is also due to _____

m. No one can believe anyone else's _____

8. Arthur then decides that there is one thing he can do.

a. Arthur gives Tom, his page, a note for _____

b. He tells Tom not to _____

c. He tells Tom to tell everyone about _____

d. He compares his ideal to _____

e. He then tells Tom not to _____

9. Arthur then falls asleep and dreams of _____

a. He remembers how _____

b. He realizes that Man is _____

c. The one species (Man) can learn from _____

d. He realizes that wars are fought over _____

    1. Boundaries are_____

    2. Mankind should keep _____

    3. But should get rid of _____

10. He realizes that one day he will _____

11. He sees that Mankind's hope lies in _____

12. He realizes that the Fate of any individual Man is _____

Part 2

Directions: After reviewing the outline of the ideas contained in chapter 14, you should realize that Arthur moves from a pessimistic outlook of life to a more optimistic one. List below, in your own words, the ideas from the outline which are pessimistic and those which are optimistic.

Pessimistic Ideas	Optimistic Ideas

Part 3

Directions: Based on your responses to the above two exercises, do you feel that the entire novel, *The Once and Future King*, is pessimistic or optimistic in its overall outlook. Support your answer with at least three reasons.

Lesson 9
The Book of Merlyn:
An Alternate Ending

Objective
- To evaluate conclusions about *The Once and Future King* in light or White's alternative ending to the novel

Notes to the Teacher
With the publication of *The Book of Merlyn* in 1977, the reader of *The Once and Future King* was given an alternate ending to the novel. Originally intended as the final book of the novel, *The Book of Merlyn* has Merlyn return to Arthur on Salisbury Plain on the evening before the final battle. There they review Arthur's lessons with the animals. The final chapter is a much more traditional "ending," telling the reader what has become of all of the major characters. It is included here in order to have students reevaluate their own opinions about the ending of the novel. Some will prefer the former ending; some will prefer this one. Whichever one the student chooses, reasons should be given for the preference.

Procedure
1. Have students read **Handout 38**.

2. Distribute **Handout 39** for students to fill out and present part 1 to the entire class. Students should add to their own lists any similarities and differences which surface in the large group. Students should then complete part 2 individually.

   A panel presenting each viewpoint could try to persuade those who are undecided, or a debate between the two sides could be presented to the rest of the class.

An Alternative Ending: *The Book of Merlyn*

Directions: T. H. White wrote *The Book of Merlyn* as an alternative ending to *The Once and Future King*. In this book Merlyn returns to Arthur on the battlefield before the battle of Salisbury Plain. He returns Arthur to the animals of Book One for some final lessons. This is the last chapter of that book.

Well, we have reached it at last, the end of our winding story.

Arthur of England went back to the world, to do his duty as well as he could. He called a truce with Mordred, having made up his mind that he must offer half his kingdom for the sake of peace. To tell the truth, he was prepared to yield it all if necessary. As a possession it had long ceased to be of value to him, and he had come to know for sure that peace was more important than a kingdom. But he felt it was his duty to retain a half if he could, and it was for this reason: that if he had even half a world to work on, he might be able still to introduce, in it, the germs of that good sense which he had learned from geese and animals.

The truce was made, the armies drawn up in their battles, face to face. Each had a standard made from a ship's mast set on wheels, at the top of which a small box held the consecrated Host, while, from the masts, there flew the banners of the Dragon and the Thistle. The knights of Mordred's party were dressed in sable armor, their plumes were sable also, and, on their arms, the scarlet whip of Mordred's badge glared with the sinister tint of blood. Perhaps they looked more terrible than they felt. It was explained to the waiting ranks that none of them must make a hostile demonstration, but all must keep their swords in sheath. Only, for fear of treachery, it was told that they might charge to rescue, if any sword was seen unharnessed at the parley.

Arthur went forward to the space between the armies with his staff, and Mordred, with his own staff in their black accoutrements, came out to meet him. They encountered, and the old king saw his son's face once again. It was taut and haggard. He too, poor man, had strayed beyond Sorrow and Solitude to the country of Kennaquhair; but he had gone without a guide and lost his way.

The treaty was agreed on, to the surprise of all, more easily than had been hoped. The king was left with half his realm. For a moment joy and peace were in the balance.

But, at that knife-edge of a moment, the old Adam reared itself in a different form. The feudal war, baronial oppression, individual might, even ideological rebellion: he had settled them all in one way or another, only to be beaten on the last lap now, by the episodic fact that man was a slayer by instinct.

A grass snake moved in the meadow near their feet, close to an officer of Mordred's staff. This officer stepped back instinctively and swung his hand across his body, his armlet with the whip showing for a second's flash. The bright sword flamed into being, to destroy the so-called viper. The waiting armies, taking it for treachery, raised their shout of rage. The lances on both sides bowed to rest. And, as King Arthur ran towards his own array, an old man with white hair trying to stem the endless tide, holding out the knuckled hands in gesture of pressing them back, struggling to the last against the flood of Might which had burst out all his life at a new place whenever he had dammed it, so the tumult rose, the war yell sounded, and the meeting waters closed above his head.

Lancelot arrived too late. He had made his best speed, but it had been in vain. All he could do was to pacify the country and give burial to the dead. Then, when a semblance of order had been restored, he hurried to Guenever. She was supposed to be in the Tower of London still, for Mordred's siege had failed.

But Guenever had gone.

In those days the rules of convents were not so strict as they are now. Often they were more like hostelries for their well-born patrons. Guenever had taken the veil at Amesbury.

She felt that they had suffered enough, and caused enough suffering to others. She refused to see her ancient lover or to talk it over. She said, which was patently untrue, that she wished to make her peace with God.

Guenever never cared for God. She was a good theologian, but that was all. The truth was that she was old and wise: she knew that Lancelot did care for God most passionately, that it was essential he should turn in that direction. So, for his sake, to make it easier for him, the great queen now renounced what she had fought for all her life, now set the example. and stood her choice. She had stepped out of the picture.

Lancelot guessed a good deal of this, and, when she refused to see him, he climbed the convent wall with Galliaging gallantry. He waylaid her to expostulate, but she was adamant and brave. Something about Mordred seemed to have broken her lust for life. They parted, never to meet on earth.

Guenever became a worldly abbess. She ruled her convent efficiently, royally, with a sort of grand contempt. The little pupils of the school were brought up in the great tradition of nobility. They saw her walking in the grounds, upright, rigid, her fingers flashing with hard rings, her linen clean and fine and scented against the rules of her order. The novices worshipped her unanimously, with schoolgirl passions, and whispered about her past. She became a Grand Old Lady. When she died at last, her Lancelot came for the body, with his snow-white hair and wrinkled cheeks, to carry it to her husband's grave. There, in the reputed grave, she was buried: a calm and regal face, nailed down and hidden in the earth.

As for Lancelot, he became a hermit in earnest. With seven of his own knights as companions he entered a monastery near Glastonbury, and devoted his life to worship. Arthur, Guenever, and Elaine were done, but his ghostly love remanied. He prayed for all of them twice a day, with all his never-beaten might, and lived in glad austerities apart from man. He even learned to distinguish bird-songs in the woods, and to have time for all the things which had been denied to him by Uncle Dap. He became and excellent gardener, and a reputed saint.

"Ipse," says a medieval poem about another old crusader, a great lord like Lancelot in his day, and one who also retired from the world:

> *Ipse post militiae cursum temporalis,*
> *Illustratus gratia doni spiritualis,*
> *Esse Christi cupiens miles specialis,*
> *In hac domo monachus factus est*
>   *claustralis.*

> He, after the bustle of temporal warfare.
> Enlightened with the grace of a spiritual gift,
> Covetous to be the special soldier of Christ,
> In this house was made a cloistered monk.
> More than usually placid, gentle and benign,
> As white as a swan on account of his old age,
> Bland and affable and lovable,

He possessed in himself the grace of the Holy Spirit,
For he often frequented Holy Church,
Joyfully listened to the mysteries of the Mass,
Proclaimed such praises as he was able,
And mentally ruminated the heavenly glory.
His gentle and jocose conversation,
Highly commendable and religious,
Was thus pleasing to the whole fraternity,
Because it was neither stuffy nor squeamish.
Here, as often as he rambled across the cloister,
He bowed from side to side to the monks,
And he saluted with a bob of his head, thus,
The ones whom he loved most intimately.
Hic per claustrum quotiens transiens meavit.
Hinc et hinc ad monchos caput inclinavit,
Hinc et hinc ad monachos caput inclinavit,
Et sic nutu capitis eos salutavit,
Quos affectu intimo plurimum amavit.

When his own death-hour came, it was accompanied by visions in the monastery. The old abbot dreamed of bells sounding most beautifully, and of angels, with happy laughter, hauling Lancelot to Heaven. They found him dead in his cell, in the act of accomplishing the third and last of his miracles. For he had died in what was called the Odor of Sanctity. When saints die, their bodies fill the room with lovely scent: perhaps of new hay, or of blossom in the spring, or of the clean seashore.

Ector pronounced his brother's keen, one of the most touching pieces of prose in the language. He said: "Ah, Lancelot, thou wert head of all Christian knights. And now I dare say, thou Sir Lancelot there thou liest, that thou were never matched of earthly knight's hand. And thou were the courtliest knight that ever bare shield. And thou were the truest friend of thy lover that ever bestrode horse. And thou were the truest lover, of a sinful man, that ever loved woman. And thou were the kindest man that ever strake with sword. And thou were the godliest person that ever came among press of knights. And thou were the meekest man and gentlest that ever ate in hall among ladies. And thou were the sternest knight to thy mortal foe that ever put spear in rest."

The Round Table had been smashed at Salisbury, its few survivors thinning out as the years went by. At last there were only four of them left: Bors the misogynist, Bleoberis, Ector, and Demaris. These old men made a pilgrimage to the Holy Land, for the repose of the souls of all their comrades, and there they died upon a Good Friday for God's sake, the last orders of the Round Table. Now there are none of them left: only knights of the Bath and of other orders degraded by comparison.

About King Arthur of England, that gentle heart and center of it all, there remains a mystery to this day. Some think that he and Mordred perished on each other's swords. Robert of Thornton mentions that he was attended by a surgeon of Salerno who found by examination of his wounds that he could never be whole again, so "he said *In manus** (boldly on the place where he lay . . .and spake no more.*" Those who adhere to this account claim that he was buried at Glastonbury, under a stone which said: HIC JACET ARTURUS REX QUONDAM REX QUE FUTURUS** and that his body was exhumed by King Henry II as a counterblast to Welsh nationalism—for the Cymry were claiming even then that

*"Into Thy Hands." The entire phrase, from the death of Jesus (Luke 23:46), is "into Thy hands, I commend my spirit."
**"Here lies Arthur, the Once and Future King.

the great king had never perished. They believed that he would come again to lead them, and they also mendaciously asserted, as usual, his British nationality. Adam of Domerham tells us, on the other hand, that the exhumation took place in April 1278, under Edward I, and that he himself was a witness of the proceedings: while it is known that a third search took place in vain under Edward III—who, by the way, revived the Round Table in 1344 as a serious order of knighthood like the Garter. Whatever the real date may have been, tradition has it that the bones when exhumed were of gigantic stature, and Guenever's had golden hair.)

Then there is another tale, widely supported, that our hero was carried away to the Vale of Affalach by a collection of queens on a magical boat. These are believed to have ferried him across the Severn to their own country, there to heal him of his wounds.

The Italians have got hold of an idea about a certain Arturo Magno who was translated to Mount Etna, where he can still be seen occasionally, they say. Don Quixote the Spaniard, a very learned gentleman, indeed went mad on account of it, maintains that he became a raven—an assertion which may not seem so wholly ridiculous to those who have read our little story. Then there are the Irish, who have muddled him up with one of the FitzGeralds and declare that he rides round in a rath, with sword upraised, to the "Londonderry Air," The Scots, who have a legend about

> *Arthur Knyght*
> *Wha raid on nycht*
> *Wi' gilten spur*
> *And candel lycht,*

still swear to him in Edinburgh, where they believe that he presides from Arthur's Seat. The Bretons claim to have heard his horn and to have seen his armor, and they also believe he will return. A book called *The High History of the Holy Grail*, which was translated by an irascible scholar called Dr. Sebastian Evans, says, on the contrary, that he was safely buried in a house of religion "that standeth at the head of the Moors Adventurous." A Miss Jessie L. Weston mentions a manuscript which she pleases to call 1533, supported by *Le Morte d'Arthur*, in which it is stated that the queen who came to carry him away was none other than the aged enchantrees morgan, his half sister, and that she took him to a magic island. Dr. Sommer regards the entire account as absurd. A lot of people called Wolfram von Eschenbach. Ulrich von Zatzikhoven, Dr. Wechssler, Professor Zimmer, Mr. Nutt, and so forth, either scout the question wholly, or remain in learned confusion. Chaucer, Spenser, Shakespeare, Milton, Wordsworth, Tennyson, and a number of other reliable witnesses agree that he is still on earth: Milton inclining to the view that he is underneath it (*Arturum-que etiam sub terris bella moventem**), while Tennyson is of the opinion that he will come again to visit us "like a modern Gentleman of stateliest port," possibly like the Prince Consort. Shakespeare's contribution is to place the beloved Falstaff, at his death, not in Abraham's but in Arthur's bosom.

The legends of the common people are beautiful, strange, and positive. Gervase of Tilbury, writing in 1212, says that, in the woods of Britain, "the foresters tell that on alternate days, about noon, or at midnight when the moon is full and shiny, they often see an array of huntsmen who, in answer to enquirers, say they are of the household and fellowship of Arthur." These, however, were probably real bands of Saxon poachers, like the followers of Robin Hood, who had named their gang in honor of the ancient king. The men of Devon are accustomed to point out "the chair and oven" of Arthur among the rocks of their

---

*"And Arthur too, stirring up wars beneath the earth."

coast. In Somersetshire there are some villages called East, and West Camel(ot), mentioned by Leland. Which are beset with legends of a king still sitting in a golden crown. It is to be noted that the river Ivel, whence, according to Drayton, our "knightly deeds and brave achievements sprong," is in the same country. So is South Cadbury, whose rector reports his parishioners as relating how "folks do say that in the night of the full moon King Arthur and his men ride around the hill, and their horses are shod with silver, and a silver shoe has been found in the track where they do ride, and when they have ridden round the hill they do stop to water their horses at the wishing well." Finally there is the little village of Bodmin in Cormwall, whose inhabitants are certain that the king inhabits a local tumulus. In 1113 they even assaulted, within the sanctuary, a party of monks from Brittany—an unheard-of thing to do—because they had thrown doubts upon the legend. It has to be admitted that some of these dates scarcely fit in with the thorny subject of Arthurian chronology, and Malory, that great man who is the noblest source of all this history, maintains a discreet reserve.

As for myself, I cannot forget the hedgehog's last farewell, coupled with Quixote's hint about the animals and Milton's subterranean dream. It is little more than a theory, but perhaps the inhabitants of Bodmin will look at their tumulus, and, if it is like an enormous molehill with a dark opening in its side, particularly if there are some badger tracks in the vicinity, we can draw our own conclusions. For I am inclined to believe that my beloved Arthur of the future is sitting at this very moment among his learned friends, in the Combination Room of the College of Life, and that they are thinking away in there for all they are worth, about the best means to help our curious species; and I for one hope that some day, when not only England but the world has need of them, and when it is ready to listen to reason, if it ever is, they will issue from their rath in joy and power; and then, perhaps, they will give us happiness in the world once more and chivalry, and the old medieval blessing of certain simple people—who tried, at any rate, in their own small way, to still the ancient brutal dream of Attila the Hun.[1]

[1]T. H. White, *The Book of Merlyn* (New York: G. P. Putnam's Son, 1978), 181–193.

The Once and Future King
Lesson 9
Handout 39

Name_____
Date_____

Comparison of Endings

Part 1
Directions: Compare the endings of *The Book of Merlyn* and "The Candle in the Wind."

Similarities	Differences

Part 2
Directions: After comparing the endings of "The Candle in the Wind" and *The Book of Merlyn*, which one do you find more satisfying? Why?

Lesson 10
Using the Legend

Objective
- To apply the ideas from *The Once and Future King* to contemporary experience

Notes to the Teacher

Too often, unfortunately, students are unable to see the relevance to the real world of something read in literature class. The cry is "That was OK, but it was just a story." And with that curt dismissal, the meaning or impact of the work leaves their lives forever. This lesson attempts to encourage students to apply some of the ideas found in the novel to contemporary experience, especially in the realm of social studies.

The excerpt from *One Brief Shining Moment* by William Manchester addresses several questions. In the first brief paragraph, he relates how several seemingly unrelated incidents tied the assassination of President John Kennedy with Arthurian legend. He then details the growth of the Arthurian legend itself. Students should be familiar with some of this material already from **Handout 4**. Finally and most importantly, he explores the growth of the Kennedy myth as an extension of the Arthurian myth.

Procedure

The teacher may wish to give some background information on the assassination of John Kennedy and its impact on the country. Distribute **Handouts 40** and **41**. Have students read the excerpt by Manchester.

During or after they have done the reading, students answer the questions on **Handout 41** and prepare to share responses in a subsequent class discussion.

The teacher may then wish to broaden the discussion by having students suggest other applications to the Arthurian legend and the ideas and concepts from the novel to the twentieth century. Some examples could be

1. The Ant Society as a model of Totalitarianism

2. The Thrashers and the Nazis

3. Parallels between the Arthurian legend and Bernard Malamud's *The Natural* (either the film or the book)

4. How a politician could change his image by associating himself with the Arthurian Legend

5. The ways in which Kennedy's association with the Arthurian legend influenced the way people think about him

These topics and others that arise in discussion can provide material for a paper, speech, or debate.

Using the Legend: John Kennedy and King Arthur

Directions: Read the following excerpt.

There were a few who sensed this at the time. Senator Ralph Yarborough had been bred in the florid tradition of southern oratory, and when the President was pronounced dead at Parkland Hospital, Yarborough turned aside, whispering, "Excalibur has sunk beneath the waves." Jackie had not heard him, but several days later, talking to Theodore H. White, she too evoked Arthurian images, remembering how Jack had loved those lines: "Don't let it be forgot/ That once there was a spot/For one brief shining moment/That was known as Camelot." Once, she said, she had thought of history as something that "bitter old men" wrote. "Then," she said, "I realized history made Jack what he was. You must think of him as this little boy, sick so much of the time, reading the Knights of the Round Table, reading Marlbourogh. For Jack, history was full of heroes— maybe other little boys will see. Men are such a combination of good and bad. Jack had this hero idea of history, the idealistic view." Other great Presidents would be elected, she said, "but there'll never be another Camelot again."

Actually, of course, there never was a Camelot. It exists only in legend. But that does not discredit it. Legends cannot be measured by dialectic. Biblical miracles are myths. If you dismissed them as lies, however, you would not only offend those who cherish them; you would also be wrong. When Jesus told Pontius Pilate that it was his mission "to bear witness to the truth" and that "everyone who is of the truth hears my voice," Pilate replied "What is truth?" Men have been struggling to answer him for two thousand years. The forest of the fourteen definitions of truth in the Oxford English dictionary is the character or disposition of being "true to a person, principle, cause, etc.; faithfulness, fidelity, loyalty, constancy, steadfast allegiance." Truth, in short, may be simple faith—faith in today's creeds; faith also in those creeds of the past which we call myths or legends. They are many. The legendary hero is found in all cultures— Vikramaditya in ancient India, for example, Siegfried of the *Nibelungenlied*, Frederick Barbarossa of the Teutons, Sigurd and Balder in Scandinavia, Cuchulain in Ireland, Arthur in Britain, and Roland in France.

Doubtless all of these champions existed in one form or another. The difficulty lies in sorting out all the facts about them. Those who shape legends have never been content to leave substance alone. Roland, for example, deserves to be remembered for his stand in Roncesvalles. His lily needs no gilding. Nevertheless, the *Chanson de Roland* tells us that he fought with a magic sword and a wonderful horn that could be heard twenty miles away, both of which he had won from a giant. This sort of fictive embroidery is even more intricate in tales of the most remarkable of all legendary heroes, Arthur of England, though here, as in so many other particulars, exceptions must be made. The embellishments—the sword in the stone, the sacred sword Excalibur, the Round Table, the Holy Grail—are so consistent with one another, and so magnificent in their entirety that they guarantee immortality in themselves. Arthur is unique. His fame is not confined to England; indeed, for several centuries he was better known on the Continent than in his own country. He is the only historic figure from England's Dark Ages to have emerged, radiant, into the Renaissance and then to have grown through the centuries that followed, until today he is as celebrated as the twentieth century's world leaders. He died 1,444 years ago. Yet his story runs through the tapestry of our literary inheritance like a golden thread, appearing in Chaucer, Malory, Spenser's *Faerie Queene*, Milton, Dryden, Fielding, Carlyle, Sir Walter Scott, Swinburne, Mark Twain, T.H. White, and John Steinbeck.

Who was he?

In the sixth century, England, no longer shielded by the Roman legions, was beset by Saxon invaders from Germany. The hordes from Saxony ("Sessoynes") were hated, and with reason: they were rapists, arsonists, carriers of disease; men who fought, as Tacitus observed, for pleasure and loot. Britons prayed for the preservation of what was left of their civilization. England had never been unified. It was a quilt of little kingdoms. The kings turned to Arthur, who was not royal himself but instead a *dux bellorum*—a military commander and cavalryman of great gifts and courage. Few records were kept in those dim, blurry centuries; fewer have survived. But some have, and they are priceless. Among those now in the British Museum are the so-called Easter Tables, contemporaneous documents prepared and updated in abbeys, and *Hisoria Brittonum*, set down by the eighth-century Welsh monk Nennius. In A.D. 488 an Easter Table reported that the English had fought a great pitched battle during which the Saxon chief had been killed. Of this clash, Nennius observes that "Arthur fought against them [the Saxons] in those days, with the kings of the Britons, but he himself was the leader of the battles."

Nennius then lists twelve Saxon defeats, all at the hands of Arthur. In the last engagement he led a charge which slew 960 Saxon. "No one overthrew them except himself alone," according to Nennius. "In all battles he stood victor." This final conflict is noted in the Easter Tables. The scribe's Easter calculations are confusing, but the year is either A.D. 499 or 518. The entry reads: "Battle of Badon, in which Arthur carried the cross of our Lord Jesus Christ on his shoulders [shield] for three days and three nights and the Britons were victors." Badon is one of the great battles in English history. The sixth-century Celtic monk Gildas, who was keeping his own record of the times, called Badon "almost the last slaughter of the enemy," and said Arthur's victory halted the Saxon advance for at least a generation. It seems incredible that anyone could have endured three days and three nights of combat, but Gildas clears that up; Badon, he says, was a siege— *"obsessio Badonici montis."* The last Easter Table citing Arthur is dated A.D. 539. It reads: "The Battle of Camlann, in which Arthur and Mordred perished."

Camlann was not a fight between Britons and Saxons. The need to drive away the Germans had united England's small kingdoms. The Saxon withdrawal had loosened the alliance. The allies quarreled with one another and then resorted to the sword. In their lethal struggle Arthur and Mordred may have been resolving a personal quarrel or championing different kingdoms. In any event only horsemen were involved; the peasants were undisturbed and unthreatened. The tremendous thing is that Arthur, by his skill and bravery, had brought Englishmen a lifetime of peace, and that was so unusual in the Dark Ages that he won what proved to be everlasting gratitude. Elizabeth Jenkins, after reviewing the brutal, almost genocidal conduct of the Saxons, writes that it "makes us see why the commander who routed them in a series of pitched battles . . . became the image of the hero and savior, whose death people refused to believe in, whose return was yearned for and expected throughout the centuries."

After the Tables, Nennius, and Gildas, the documentary trail is faint. But we must remember that during those ages only monks could read and write. Even kings were illiterate. Nevertheless, men could speak. Thus, Arthur's story is spread. Tales told by the fireside doubtless gained in the telling. By the tenth century it was assumed that Arthur had been a king, which he never was. Detailed accounts of his life did not appear until the early 1100s, and it is impossible to sort out the apocrypha in them, or to determine what was omitted. They carry no mention of Guinevere, for example. Yet she lived, and there can be little dispute over why she was remembered. To this day, in remote Welsh villages, a woman who breaks her marriage vows is called "a regular Guinevere."

In 1184 fire destroyed the last structure dating from Arthur's time, a small fifth-century wattle-and-daub church—the first Christian shrine in England—where he may have prayed before going into battle. Meanwhile, however, the Arthurian legend continued to grow, and not only in England. The prior of Tewkesbury noted that British pilgrims, returning from abroad, reported "winged praise of Arthur" in Egypt, the Bosporus, Carthage, Antioch, Armenia, and all the major cities of western Europe. Over the next two centuries writers added Lancelot and the Round Table—actually peasants had spoken of *Morte d 'Arthur,* establishing for all time the image of the noble king presiding over his chivalrous knights and slowly realizing that Camelot and all it represented were doomed because two people he cherished most, his beautiful wife and his mightiest knight, had become lovers. After a great convulsion of violence Lancelot vanished, Guinevere closed her legs and entered a nunnery, Excalibur went its watery way, and Arthur departed to sleep beneath the inscription *"Hic jacet Arturus, Rex quondam, Rexque futurus"*—"Here lies Arthur, the Once and Future King." Thus, he joined that small circle of mythical heroes who can never die, who, in Steinbeck's words, have found "a seat of worth beyond the reach of envy, whose occupant ceases to be a man and becomes the receptacle of the wishful longings of the world."

Arthur lived, fought, and died when all his countrymen, including monks and nuns, believed in heroes. Kennedy's age was the age of the antihero, the victim. Alienation had become a cultural vogue. Great leaders belonged to the past; the leonine mold had been broken. It therefore followed that this young President who seemed to have been cast from it must be an imposter. Those who held this view were a minority, but they were immensely influential. Because of Kennedy's class, taste, and interest in the world of ideas, he had moved among them for years. Their modes were familiar to him but unacceptable. He continued to write of the gallantry they disparaged and spoke eloquently of the need for a new idealism. In Houston, the night before he was slain, he quoted the Proverbs: "Where there is no vision, the people perish." He saw his county threatened by a gray tide of mediocrity and an implacable enmity toward the concept of excellence which he exalted.

In his lifetime this was not always understood. His elegance, his sophistication, and his self-depreciating wit were effective camouflage. He needed that; he was a man of understatement. Nevertheless, the one illness which never afflicted him was cloying liberal piety. He felt neither alienated nor victimized. Duty, dedication, and devotion were the very essence of him, and if those words sound quaint, the fault lies with us and not with him. "Unless democracy can produce able leaders," he had written at Harvard in 1940, "its chances of survival are slight." That thought became his keel. He seemed taller that he was because he was reaching; and because he would never stop reaching, his grasp became extraordinary.

The tension between him and the intellectuals who should have identified with his presidency but didn't, became irrelevant in Dallas. Most Americans didn't know that heroism was obsolete. Their grief in November 1963 was like that of any people, at any time in history, whose champion has been slain. During the seventy-four-hour, fifty-four-minute telethon some seventy million people watched their TV screens averaging nearly ten hours at a stretch. They were stricken. Some have never fully recovered. Some institutions are universal, and burial of the dead is one, but it can be done in various ways. The ritualistic splendor of these mourning ceremonies for Kennedy struck deep, atavistic chords, recalling ancestral memories older than the nation. For example, the riderless, caparisoned steed that followed the gun carriage, with boots reversed in their stirrups, a sign that the beloved rider would ride no more, goes back at least to the days of Ghengis Kahn and Tamerlane. Somehow Jack's young widow had reached back across the centuries and found the noblest of funeral rites, celebrating the sacrifice of fallen leaders; then, gathering that solemn aura into the prism of her own anguish, she refracted it into a radiant, penetrating beam of light that blinded a nation with its own tears.

One conclusion was predictable. The country's concept of President Kennedy had changed forever. Once a leader becomes a martyr, transformation naturally follows. Endowed with a nimbus, he must also be clothed in raiment which he would have found strange, but which satisfies the public eye. As Edmund Wilson pointed out, the Lincoln to whom Americans are introduced as children, and whom Carl Sandburg did so much to perpetuate, has little in common with the cool, aloof genius who ruled this nation unflinchingly as the sixteenth President of the United States. That man was destroyed on the evening of April 14, 1865. The urbane public man who became his nineteenth successor shared his fate. The real Kennedy vanished on November 22, 1963. The fact that Lincoln and Kennedy shared an abiding faith in a government of laws therefore becomes inconsequential; legends, because they are essentially tribal, override such details. What the hero was and what he believed are submerged by the demands of those who mourn him. In myth he becomes what they want him to have been, and anyone who belittles this transformation has an imperfect understanding of how the emotions of an entire nation may be moved. A romantic concept of what may have been can be far more compelling than what was. "Love is very penetrating," Santayana observed, "but it penetrates to possibilities, rather than to facts." All people ask of a legendary hero is that he may have been truly noble, a splendid figure who was cherished and cruelly lost. Glorification follows. In love, nations are no less generous than individuals, In grief, they are no less stricken. And as the years pass their loyalty deepens.

The legendary Arthur, like the Jack Kennedy we knew, was in his element on seas and streams. He was said to have been conceived at Tintagel, where towering seas crash against cliffs and burst into billowing clouds of foam. Five of the great battles in which he rescued England from the swarming Saxon invaders were fought on the banks of rivers; he fell with his last wound on the shore of another stream; he returned his sacred sword to the Lady of the Lake, whose hand rose from the depths to receive it; and he was carried away be three queens on a royal barge.

But those who yearn for his strength and courage do not look seaward. Since the beginning of time men have sought the answer to profound mysteries in the sky. In various eras stars have been worshiped. Along the Euphrates, observations of them were recorded before 3800 B.C.; the Chinese had discovered the 365 $1/4$-day solar year by 2300 B.C.; the Egyptians laid out their pyramids and established the rules of surveying by charting celestial movements. Thus, those who seek Arthur search the stellar vault of the heavens, seeing him in Arcturus, the star said to have been named for him, or in the sparkling constellation Ursa Major, "Arthur's Wain."

If you were sitting beside Jim Swindal in the Air Force One cockpit during that flight home from Texas on November 22, hurtling eastward at a velocity approaching the speed of sound, goaded by a mighty tailwind, you became aware that night was approaching rapidly. Less than forty-five minutes after you left Dallas, shadows began to thicken over eastern Arkansas. In the southern sky you could see a waif on a moon, a day and a half off the quarter, hanging ghostlike near the meridian. Like you, Jim, near tears, was fighting to control himself. Conversation was out of the question; voices couldn't be trusted. Outside, twilight turned to olive gloaming and became dusk. You looked out upon the overarching sky and realized that in the last days of autumn the northern firmament is brilliant. Jupiter lay over the Carolinas, the Big Dipper beyond Chicago. Cassiopeia and the great square of Pegasus twinkled overhead. Arcturus was setting redly over Kansas. But the brightest light in the bruise-blue canopy was Capella, just beginning its annual five-month wintry cruise over the hemisphere. Always a star of the first magnitude, it seemed dazzling tonight, and as Air Force One rocketed toward West Virginia it rose majestically a thousand miles to the northeast, over Boston. Ever since then you have thought of Capella as Kennedy's star. It is brilliant, it is swift, it soars. Of course, to see it, you must lift your eyes. But he showed us how to do that.[1]

[1]William Manchester, *One Brief Shining Moment: Remembering Kennedy* (New York: Little Brown & Co.), 1983.

Name_____
Date_____

Using the Legend: Kennedy and Arthur

Directions: After reading the excerpt from *One Brief Shining Moment* by William Manchester, answer the following questions.

1. How did the connection between Kennedy and Arthur begin following Kennedy's death?

2. How is Manchester's idea about Arthur similar or different from T. H. White's?

3. For Manchester what does Arthur represent?

4. In what ways has Kennedy's association with Arthur helped Kennedy's reputation?

5. According to Manchester, what is the difference between the culture that began the legends of Arthur and the culture of Kennedy's years?

6. What does Manchester conclude that Kennedy taught us to do?

7. In what ways is this similar to T.H. White's view of what Arthur has done, or at least what the legend about Arthur has done?

Name_____

Date_____

Reading Guide Questions
"The Sword in the Stone"

1. What does Sir Grummore suggest that Sir Ector should find for the boys?

2. What ways does he suggest to go about getting one?

3. Why, according to Arthur, should he and Kay not take Cully out?

4. What happens to Cully while Arthur and Kay take him hunting?

5. What is Kay's response?

6. What is Arthur's response?

7. Name some things Arthur is afraid of when he is alone in the woods.

8. Why is King Pellinore afraid of the woods?

9. Describe the Questing Beast.

10. What does Merlyn look like?

11. What does Merlyn mean when he tells Arthur that he "lives backward in time"?

12. Who is Archimedes?

13. What animal does Merlyn change Arthur into?

14. What does Mr. P. tell Arthur about Might?

15. What happens to the arrow that Arthur shoots straight up into the air after he and Kay play Rovers?

16. How does Merlyn show Arthur what jousting is really like?

17. How does King Pellinore win the joust with Sir Grummore?

18. What does Grummore ask Pellinore to do when they have finished jousting?

19. What are the two "ordeals" that Arthur must go through as a hawk in the mews?

20. Why do Kay and Arthur fight on the next day?

21. What is Merlyn's answer to Arthur when he is asked why Kay does not get the same special education?

22. Whom do Arthur and Kay meet in their adventure in the Forest Sauvage?

23. What has happened to Friar Tuck, Wat, the Dog Boy, and Cavall?

24. Why is it necessary that Arthur and Kay rescue the prisoners in Castle Chariot?

25. What does the Griffin look like?

26. What is Castle Chariot made of?

27. What happens when they confront Morgan La Fay with the iron?

28. Who kills the Griffin?

29. What happens to Arthur?

30. What are the only two words that ants have to describe things?

31. What is Arthur's job in the ant colony?

32. What happens when an ant from another colony crosses into the nest where Arthur is?

33. Why is William Twyti coming to the Castle of the Forest Sauvage?

34. What are some of the ways in which the people of the castle celebrate Christmas?

35. What has happened to the Questing Beast?

36. Why has it happened?

37. What reasons does Arthur give for choosing the Rook as his favorite bird?

38. What are Merlyn's and Archimedes' favorite birds?

39. According to Merlyn what are the origins of bird language?

40. Why is Kay's announcement that he was late for his lesson because he killed a Thrush, ironic?

41. What does Arthur learn from his being turned into an owl?

42. What is Lyo-Lyok's reaction when Arthur asks her if Geese ever fight each other?

43. Why are there no boundaries for a Goose?

44. When Arthur confesses that he likes fighting, what does Lyo-Lyok say is the reason?

45. What do the Wild Geese do while flying over the North Sea?

46. What does Arthur learn about Goose society?

47. After six years pass, what is about to happen to Kay?

48. What will happen to Arthur?

49. What animal is Arthur turned into the last time?

50. Why does Arthur (as the badger) not kill the hedgehog?

51. What does the badger tell Arthur about Man?

52. What news does Pellinore bring when he arrives for Kay's knighting?

53. How will the new King be determined?

54. What news does Arthur have to tell Sir Ector?

55. What happens to Kay as he is on the way to the tournament in London?

56. Why can Arthur not get Kay's sword?

57. Where does Arthur find a sword for Kay?

58. What is Arthur's reaction to Ector and Kay's kneeling to him?

59. Why do the people accept Arthur as King?

60. Who reappears to help Arthur become a good King?

Name_____

Date_____

Reading Guide Questions
"The Queen of Air and Darkness"

1. According to the Orkney brothers, what happened to their "granny," Igraine?

2. While the boys tell this story, what is their mother, Morgause, doing?

3. Why does Merlyn tell Arthur that the battle was not as "splendid" as he (Arthur) thought it was?

4. According to Merlyn, why are the "Gaels" fighting the "Galls"?

5. What are the personal reasons that Lot is engaging in this war?

6. According to Merlyn, what is the only reason for fighting a war?

7. Apart form aggression, what is the other reason that men like to fight, according to Merlyn?

8. Where does St. Toirdealbhach, Mother Morlan's guest, come from? What is he?

9. What do the Orkney brothers do after leaving Mother Morlan's house?

10. Who arrives at the shore when the Orkney brothers get there? How do they arrive?

11. Why does Merlyn send Arthur away from his tower room?

12. How does Arthur repay Merlyn for this?

13. What is Arthur's idea for a new order of chivalry?

14. Why is King Pellinore depressed?

15. What is the only way to capture the unicorn?

16. What do the Orkney brothers do with the unicorn after Agravaine kills it?

17. What is Morgause's reaction to the unicorn?

18. How does Arthur propose to eliminate jealousy in his new order of chivalry?

19. How does Merlyn suggest he can get one of these?

20. What does Kay suggest is a good reason to start a war?

21. What does Merlyn say that Jesus did?

22. How do Grummore and Palomides plan to cheer up King Arthur?

23. What does Agravaine do in the fight with Gawaine?

24. What lesson does the parable about the man who ran away from Death teach?

25. What does Merlyn tell Arthur will be written on Arthur's tomb?

26. What does Arthur ask Merlyn about the future?

27. Who arrives as Pellinore is trying to rescue Grummore and Palomides from the Questing Beast?

28. What announcement does St. Toirdealbhach make?

29. What is the traditional way of fighting which Lot and the eleven kings propose to use in the Battle of Bedegraine?

30. What are the "atrocities" that Arthur commits in this battle?

31. Who are Ban and Bors? What role do they play in the battle?

32. What is a spancel? What "magic" does it have?

33. What do the Orkney brothers vow before they leave for England?

34. What is it that Merlyn realizes he forgot to tell Arthur?

35. Who is Mordred?

Reading Guide Questions
"The Ill-Made Knight"

1. Why does Lancelot begin his vigorous physical training program?

2. Why does Lancelot call himself "the ill-made knight"?

3. What does Lancelot learn from Uncle Dap?

4. In addition to being Arthur's "best knight," what else does Lancelot want to be able to do?

5. What does Lancelot learn from Merlyn on his visit to the castle?

6. What is Lancelot's reaction to this news?

7. With whom does Lancelot joust at the ford near Camelot?

8. What makes Lancelot realize that Guenever is a real person?

9. Who are the first two people to realize that Lancelot and Guenever are in love?

10. How does Arthur handle the problem?

11. What is the most valuable of Lancelot's possessions?

12. What does Lancelot ask Arthur on their return from the war?

13. Who takes Lancelot prisoner at Castle Chariot?

14. Who are the various knights whom Lancelot fights on his quest?

15. What two incidents which happen to Lancelot show the old ways of Might fighting against Arthur's new order of chivalry?

16. To whom does Lancelot have all of his prisoners surrender?

17. What is this person's reaction?

18. What has Arthur's ideal turned into?

19. What are the reasons that Lancelot cannot give into his love for Guenever?

20. What miracle does Lancelot perform at Corbin?

21. How does Elaine trick Lancelot into sleeping with her?

22. Why does Lancelot now feel that he does not have to restrain his love for Guenever anymore?

23. What does Arthur do to give Lancelot and Guenever a full year together?

24. What does Lancelot tell Guenever he has given up for her?

25. What news does Sir Bors bring to court?

26. What is Guenever's reaction to this news?

27. What does Elaine plan to do?

28. How does Arthur handle the situation between Lancelot and Guenever?

29. What does Guenever forbid Lancelot to do while Elaine is at court?

30. How does Elaine trick Lancelot again?

31. What happens to Lancelot when Guenever and Elaine fight over him?

32. After two years, what do most people believe about Lancelot?

33. What adventures does Sir Bliant's "wild man" have that suggest that he is Lancelot?

34. How does King Pelles use the "wild man" who comes to Corbin?

35. What has happened to Elaine since Lancelot's disappearance?

36. Who is Galahad? What kind of child is he?

37. What name does Lancelot give himself when he and Elaine go to live at Castle Bliant?

38. What various meanings does this name have?

39. What happens when they hold a tournament at Castle Bliant?

40. What are Lancelot's new arms?

41. Who shows up at Castle Bliant to persuade Lancelot to return to Camelot?

42. Who is the one who finally persuades Lancelot to leave?

43. In what ways has Arthur's dream been a success?

44. Who kills Morgause and why?

45. Who kills Lamorak? How?

46. What idea does Arthur have in order to channel Might, now that there is order in his kingdom?

47. What does Lancelot suggest that they search for?

48. Why can Gawaine not successfully find the Grail?

49. What are the two things that Ector and Gawaine lack that prohibits them from completing the quest?

50. What are the tests Bors is put to on his quest?

51. What happens when Lionel is about to kill Bors?

52. Why does Aglovale want to fight Gawaine?

53. How do Aglovale and Percivale's sister die?

54. Why is Percivale allowed to find the Grail?

55. What is Lancelot's reaction when he finds out that he is no longer the "best knight"?

56. What is the one sin Lancelot does not at first confess, which he realizes after he is defeated for a second time?

57. What does Lancelot see when he arrives at Carbonek?

58. What reasons does Lancelot give Guenever for not returning to their old love?

59. What four "phases" has the court of Camelot gone through?

60. Why does Sir Mador accuse the queen of treason?

61. Why does the queen have difficulty finding a champion?

62. What new idea does Arthur have for getting rid of Might altogether?

63. Why is Lancelot involved in an "Eternal Quadrangle"?

64. What does Elaine believe when Lancelot returns to Corbin?

65. What does Lancelot wear at the tournament at Corbin?

66. What does Elaine do when she realizes that Lancelot will not be staying at Corbin?

67. What happens to Guenever when she is out A-Maying?

68. How does Lancelot arrive to rescue Guenever?

69. What does Guenever do to win Lancelot's love again?

70. Why does Meliagrance accuse the queen of treason?

71. How does Meliagrance trick Lancelot?

72. What is the only way that Meliagrance will fight with Lancelot after he is unhorsed?

73. Why does Sir Urre come to Camelot?

74. Who is the only knight who can help Sir Urre?

75. What effect does this have on the other members of the Round Table?

Name_____

Date_____

Reading Guide Questions
"The Candle in the Wind"

1. What do both Agravaine and Mordred want to tell Arthur?

2. Why does Agravaine want to do it?

3. Why does Mordred want to do it?

4. Why can Mordred not accuse Arthur publicly?

5. What is Agravaine's plan?

6. What is the reaction of Gawaine, Gaheris, and Gareth to the plan of Agravaine and Mordred?

7. What happens when Gawaine threatens to stop Mordred?

8. In what way is this similar to an earlier incident in the lives of the Orkney brothers?

9. What stops the fight?

10. How is Arthur's kingdom described in chapter 3?

11. What does Guenever refuse Lancelot while Arthur is at Camelot?

12. What does Lancelot want them to do?

13. What happens while they discuss this?

14. How does Arthur make them aware of his presence?

15. What secret does Arthur tell Lancelot and Guenever?

16. What warning does he give them?

17. What does he make Lancelot promise not to do?

18. When Arthur enters the Justice Room, what do Gawaine, Gaheris, and Gareth do?

19. What do Mordred and Agravaine do?

20. What is Arthur's response?

21. What does Mordred suggest that Arthur do so that their accusation can be proved?

22. What is Arthur's response?

23. Why does Gareth come to Lancelot's room?

24. Why does Lancelot not believe him?

25. When Lancelot goes to Guenever's room, what does he forget?

26. What is Guenever's response when Lancelot tells her of Gareth's warning?

27. What makes her change her mind?

28. Once they are trapped, what does Lancelot tell Guenever he will do?

29. Who does Lancelot kill and why?

30. What do we find out that Lancelot did to escape?

31. Why did he not kill Mordred?

32. What is going to happen to Guenever?

33. Why do Gareth and Gaheris go unarmed to guard the queen?

34. What happens as Guenever is to be burned at the stake?

35. What news does Mordred bring to Arthur and Gawaine after the battle?

36. Why does Arthur beseige Joyous Guard six months later?

37. Why does Lancelot refuse to fight?

38. What happens when he does go out to fight?

39. Who are The Thrashers?

40. What is Guenever's idea for peace?

41. What is Lancelot's response to Gawaine's charges of murder?

42. What is Lancelot's punishment?

43. What does Guenever vow to do?

44. What does Lancelot vow to Arthur?

45. According to Guenever, why did Arthur go with Gawaine to fight Lancelot?

46. What happens when Gawaine and Lancelot fight?

47. What has happened to Arthur?

48. Why did Arthur have to leave Mordred as Lord Protector of England?

49. What lie does Mordred intend to spread and why?

50. What does Mordred then intend to do in order to "complete the pattern"?

51. What happens to Gawaine the second time he tries to fight Lancelot?

52. According to her letter, why did Guenever agree to marry Mordred?

53. What weapon does Mordred use to beseige the Tower of London?

54. Why do the English give up the seige of the French so suddenly?

55. What has happened to Gawaine?

56. What does Gawaine ask Lancelot to do?

57. On the eve of the battle, why is Arthur saddened when he thinks about his life?

58. Why does Arthur tell Tom, his page, not to fight in the battle?

59. To what does Arthur compare his ideal of knighthood and chivalry?

60. What, in the end, does Arthur realize about War as he remembers his education with the animals?

Name_____

Date_____

Quiz 1—"The Sword in the Stone"—Chapters 1–11

Multiple Choice
Directions: On the lines provided, write the letter of the best answer.

____ 1. King Pellinore, whom the Wart meets in the Forest Sauvage, is hunting for
a. a unicorn
b. a brachet
c. a boar
d. the Questing Beast

____ 2. Merlyn lives
a. backward in time
b. forwards in time like everyone else
c. outside of time
d. sideways of time

____ 3. When Merlyn turns Wart into a fish, he is almost eaten by
a. Merlyn
b. Mr. P., the King of the Moat
c. a shark
d. a fisherman

____ 4. The arrow which Wart shoots straight up into the air is
a. lost in the forest
b. taken by Robin Hood
c. grabbed by a crow
d. changed by Merlyn

____ 5. When Wart spends the night in the mews as a merlin, he must answer certain questions and
a. kill a mouse
b. stand next to Cully
c. fly around the mews
d. challenge the leader to a fight

____ 6. When Merlyn sends Wart and Kay on an Adventure in the Forest Sauvage, they meet
a. King Uther
b. King Pellinore
c. Sir Grummore
d. Robin Hood and his men

____ 7. Wart, Dog Boy, Friar Tuck and Cavall, the hound, have all been taken prisoner in the Castle Chariot by
a. Merlyn
b. Robin Hood
c. Morgan La Fay
d. King Uther

____ 8. Castle Chariot is protected and guarded by a
a. griffin
b. unicorn
c. knight in black armor
d. sword bridge

____ 9. Castle Chariot appears to be made of
a. stone
b. food
c. gold
d. silver

____ 10. In order to win the joust with Sir Grummore, King Pellinore
a. asks Merlyn for help
b. cheats
c. has Wart and Kay help him
d. uses the Questing Beast to scare him

Name_____

Date_____

Quiz 2—"The Sword in the Stone"—Chapters 12–24

Multiple Choice
Directions: On the lines provided, write the letter of the best answer.

____ 1. When Merlyn transforms Arthur into an ant, Arthur discovers that ants have only two ways of describing things. They are
   a. Ant and Not Ant
   b. Good and Not Good
   c. Done and Not Done
   d. Yes and No

____ 2. The ants go to war because
   a. the nest was attacked by another animal
   b. the ant from another nest wanders into their nest
   c. some ants decide to revolt against the government
   d. they discover Arthur is not really an ant

____ 3. Sir Ector receives a letter form King Uther telling him to expect William Twyti who will arrive at Christmas to
   a. hunt in the Forest Sauvage
   b. take Arthur back to court
   c. inspect Ector's lands
   d. recruit men for the army

____ 4. When Pellinore finds the Questing Beast, she is
   a. killing a boar
   b. fighting with a hunting dog
   c. sick because of his neglect
   d. playing with Arthur

____ 5. Merlyn says that the origin of bird language is
   a. imitation
   b. a mystery
   c. a need for music
   d. the need for survival

____ 6. When Arthur, as a wild goose, suggests to Lyo-Lyok that geese fight each other, she is
   a. amused
   b. angry and horrified
   c. pleased
   d. ready to tell him a story

____ 7. After six years go by, the Castle of the Forest Sauvage is preparing for the knighting of
   a. Sir Ector
   b. Merlyn
   c. Arthur
   d. Kay

____ 8. The last animal that Merlyn turns Arthur into is a
   a. hedgehog
   b. skunk
   c. badger
   d. beaver

____ 9. When Pellinore arrives at the castle for the knighting, he brings news of the death of
   a. King Uther
   b. Robin Wood
   c. the Questing Beast
   d. Merlyn

____ 10. When Kay forgets his sword for the tournament in London, Arthur brings him
   a. a wooden sword
   b. his sword from the inn where they are staying
   c. King Pellinore's wooden sword
   d. the sword from the stone and anvil in the churchyard

Name_____

Date_____

Quiz 3—"The Queen of Air and Darkness"

Multiple Choice
Directions: On the lines provided, write the letter of the best answer.

____ 1. The youngest of the Orkney brothers is
   a. Gawaine
   b. Agravaine
   c. Gaheris
   d. Gareth

____ 2. In order to create a small magic to become invisible, Morgause
   a. boils a live cat
   b. kills a bird
   c. weaves a cloak
   d. uses the venom of a snake

____ 3. Merlyn tells Arthur that the war against Lot was not "splendid" because
   a. Arthur was wounded
   b. Merlyn was wounded
   c. 700 men were killed
   d. Arthur broke Excalibur, his sword

____ 4. According to Merlyn, the only reason for fighting a war is
   a. land
   b. because someone else starts it
   c. fame
   d. to impose an idea on someone else

____ 5. The Irish, whiskey drinking monk who tells the Orkney brothers fantastic stories is
   a. St. Toirdealbhach
   b. Mother Morlan
   c. Palomides
   d. Conor MacNessa

____ 6. Pellinore, Grummore, and Palomides arrive in Scotland on
   a. donkeys
   b. a magic barge
   c. horses
   d. foot

____ 7. Arthur has the idea of starting a new order of chivalry which will
   a. use no weapons
   b. fight in wars all over the world
   c. use Might only for Right
   d. fight only each other

____ 8. King Pellinore is in love with
   a. the Questing Beast
   b. Queen Morgause
   c. Maid Marion
   d. the Queen of Flander's Daughter

____ 9. The unicorn is killed by
   a. Gawaine
   b. Agravaine
   c. Gareth
   d. Gaheris

____ 10. In order to eliminate jealousy among his knights, Arthur proposes that they all
   a. wear the same color armor
   b. sit at a round table
   c. take turns sitting at the head of the table
   d. carry blank shields

____ 11. Grummore and Palomides plan to cheer up Pellinore by
   a. dressing up as the Questing Beast
   b. taking him back to Flanders
   c. finding another girl for him
   d. throwing a party for him

____ 12. Merlyn tells Arthur that his tomb will contain the following epitaph:
   a. Here lies Arthur, England's greatest king
   b. Here lies Arthur, founder of the Round Table
   c. Here lies Arthur, the Once and Future King
   d. Here lies Arthur, Merlyn's favorite student

____ 13. The Questing Beast falls in love with
   a. Morgause
   b. Mother Morlan
   c. Piggy
   d. the fake Questing Beast with Grummore and Palomides inside

____ 14. In the Battle of Bedegraine, Arthur and
his army are aided by
a. Ban and Bors
b. Gareth and Gawaine
c. Lancelot and Leodegrand
d. Lot and the eleven kings

____ 15. Mordred is
a. Merlyn's son
b. Ban's son
c. Lancelot's son
d. Arthur's son

True-False
Directions: Write the word on the line.

_____ 16. St. Toirdealbhach marries
Mother Morlan.

_____ 17. In a fight with his brother
Gawaine, Agravaine pulls a
small knife on him.

_____ 18. Morgause is impressed with her
sons after they kill the Unicorn
for her.

_____ 19. Merlyn realizes that the thing
he forgot to tell Arthur was the
way that he will die.

_____ 20. The nickname for the Queen of
Flander's daughter is Piggy.

Quiz 4—"The Ill-Made Knight"—Chapters 1–24

Multiple Choice
Directions: On the lines provided, write the letter of the best answer.

____ 1. Physically, Lancelot can be described as
  a. handsome
  b. ugly
  c. weak
  d. good looking

____ 2. In addition to being Arthur's best knight, Lancelot would like to
  a. be able to perform a miracle
  b. be able to see the future
  c. be able to go on a crusade
  d. be able to fight the devil

____ 3. Lancelot falls in love with Guenever because
  a. she is beautiful
  b. she immediately loves him
  c. he has hurt her
  d. she is Arthur's queen

____ 4. The most valuable of Lancelot's possessions is his
  a. sword
  b. horse
  c. lance
  d. word

____ 5. Lancelot is taken prisoner by four evil queens and locked up at
  a. Camelot
  b. Carbonek
  c. Castle Chariot
  d. Castle Bliant

____ 6. Lancelot saves Elaine from
  a. a boiling bath
  b. an evil knight
  c. a magic spear
  d. a devil

____ 7. The son of Lancelot and Elaine is
  a. Percivale
  b. Bors
  c. Gawaine
  d. Galahad

____ 8. Caught between the trickery of Elaine and the accusations of Guenever, Lancelot
  a. leaves for France
  b. goes mad
  c. kills Elaine
  d. kills himself

____ 9. King Pelles takes in the "wild man" who appears at Corbin to make him his
  a. squire
  b. kitchen servant
  c. fool
  d. daughter's husband

____ 10. The name that Lancelot gives himself while living at Castle Bliant can mean
  a. The Ugly Knight
  b. The Knight Who Has Done Wrong
  c. The Ill-Starred Knight
  d. all of these

Quiz 5-"The Ill-Made Knight"—Chapters 25–45

Multiple Choice
Directions: On the lines provided, write the letter of the best answer.

____ 1. Morgause, like the unicorn in the previous book, is killed by
   a. Gawaine
   b. Agravaine
   c. Gareth
   d. Mordred

____ 2. Mordred kills Sir Lamorak by
   a. killing him in a joust
   b. stabbing him in the back
   c. poisoning his food
   d. cutting off his head

____ 3. When Arthur suggests that the knights need to be set against a spiritual goal, Lancelot suggests that they search for
   a. The Grail
   b. an angel
   c. a saint
   d. a holy sword

____ 4. Perceval's sister dies because she gives up her blood to save
   a. her brother
   b. Lancelot
   c. a lady who has leprosy
   d. Arthur

____ 5. Lancelot refuses to become Guenever's lover again because
   a. she is too old
   b. he is afraid of Arthur
   c. he has found a woman he loves more
   d. he has seen the Grail

____ 6. Sir Mador accuses the queen of treason when at a dinner party given by her, it is discovered that
   a. the apples are poisined
   b. she is Lancelot's lover
   c. she tried to kill the king
   d. she seduced Gareth

____ 7. When she realizes that Lancelot will not stay at Corbin, Elaine
   a. joins a convent
   b. tries to kill Lancelot
   c. kills herself
   d. tries to kill Guenever

____ 8. When Guenever goes a-Maying, Sir Meliagrance
   a. goes along with her
   b. vows to protect her from attackers
   c. sets up an ambush and captures her
   d. kills her attackers and saves her

____ 9. Sir Meliagrance agrees to fight Sir Lancelot only when Lancelot agrees to
   a. wear no armor on his left side
   b. carry no shield
   c. have his left hand tied behind him
   d. all of these

____ 10. Sir Urre can have his wounds healed only by
   a. King Arthur
   b. the best knight in the world
   c. a wizard
   d. a holy woman

Name_____

Date_____

Quiz 6—"The Candle in the Wind"

Multiple Choice
Directions: On the lines provided, write the letter of the best answer.

_____ 1. Agravaine and Mordred want to make a direct accusation to Arthur about
   a. Arthur's father
   b. the killing of their mother
   c. Lancelot and Quenever
   d. Arthur's attempted murder of Mordred

_____ 2. Arthur tells Lancelot and Guenever that
   a. he is Mordred's father
   b. he tried to have Mordred killed
   c. Mordred will try to get at him through them
   d. all of these

_____ 3. Once the accusation has been made, Arthur tells Mordred and Agravaine that if they can not prove it, he will
   a. use the law to prosecute them
   b. forget the whole incident
   c. kill them both himself
   d. banish them from England

_____ 4. In his attempt to escape from Guenever's room, Lancelot kills
   a. Mordred
   b. Agravaine
   c. Arthur
   d. Guenever

_____ 5. As a result of having Lancelot caught in her room, Guenever has been sentenced to be
   a. hanged
   b. shot
   c. banished from England
   d. burned at the stake

_____ 6. In his rescue of Guenever, Lancelot kills
   a. Gaheris and Gareth
   b. Mordred and Arthur
   c. Gawaine and Mordred
   d. Gawaine and Guenever

_____ 7. Mordred's group of knights and followers are called
   a. Nazis
   b. Thrashers
   c. Galls
   d. Gawaines

_____ 8. Guenever says that the only person who can create a peace between Arthur and Lancelot is
   a. Mordred
   b. Gawaine
   c. the Pope
   d. the King of France

_____ 9. After peace is made, Lancelot is
   a. exiled to France
   b. welcomed back to Camelot
   c. killed by Gawaine
   d. burned at the stake

_____ 10. When Arthur goes to France with Gawaine, Mordred is
   a. put into prison
   b. asked to go with them
   c. made Lord Protector
   d. poisoned by Guenever

_____ 11. Mordred intends to spread the lie that
   a. Guenever is dead
   b. Lancelot and Arthur are dead
   c. he is Arthur's son
   d. he has killed Lancelot

_____ 12. Mordred tells Guenever that he intends to
   a. kill her
   b. imprison her
   c. marry her
   d. exile her

_____ 13. When Guenever blockades herself in the Tower of London, Mordred attacks the Tower with
   a. bombs
   b. Robin Hood's men
   c. flaming swords
   d. cannon

____ 14. Lancelot receives a letter asking him to help Arthur fight Mordred, from
   a. Guenever
   b. Gawaine
   c. Arthur himself
   d. the Pope

____ 15. Tom, of Newbold Revell near Warwick, is Arthur's
   a. page
   b. son
   c. brother
   d. new teacher

True-False
Directions: Write the word on the line.

_____ 16. Lancelot is warned of the treachery of Mordred and Agravaine by Gawaine.

_____ 17. Agravaine and Mordred accuse Lancelot and Guenever of adultery in front of Arthur in the Justice Room.

_____ 18. Arthur, in an attempt to kill Mordred, was responsible for the death of many babies.

_____ 19. Arthur tells Tom of Newbold Revell that he must fight to the death in the upcoming battle near Salisbury.

_____ 20. At the end, Arthur realizes that most wars are fought over imaginary borders.

Name_____

Date_____

Final Test

Part 1—Matching—1 point each
Directions: On the lines provided, write the best answer.

____ 1. Mordred

____ 2. King Pellinore

____ 3. Wart

____ 4. Lyo-Lyok

____ 5. Morgause

____ 6. Kay

____ 7. Agravaine

____ 8. Galahad

____ 9. St. Toirdealbhach

____ 10. Sir Grummore

____ 11. Piggy

____ 12. Uncle Dap

____ 13. Le Chevalier Mal Fet

____ 14. Gawaine

____ 15. Elaine

____ 16. Guenever

____ 17. Merlyn

____ 18. Tom of Newbold Revell

____ 19. King Uther

____ 20. The Thrashers

A. Mother of the Orkney brothers

B. The Queen of Flanders' daughter, later married to Pellinore

C. Arthur's father

D. Leader of the ant colony

E. Arthur's childhood name

F. The fish who is King of the Moat

G. Arthur's page

H. Rescued from the boiling water by Lancelot

I. Arthur's wife and Lancelot's lover

J. Teacher of the Orkney brothers

K. Arthur's foster brother

L. Uther's Master of the Hunt

M. Mordred's followers

N. Kills the unicorn

O. Real name of Robin Hood

P. With Palomides, dresses up as the Questing Beast

Q. Arthur's illegitimate son

R. A wild goose

S. Arthur's teacher

T. Lancelot's son

U. Guenever's child

V. Name taken by Lancelot

W. Searches for the Questing Beast

X. Arthur's mother

Y. Oldest of the Orkney brothers

Z. Lancelot's teacher

Name_____

Date_____

Part 2—Fill in the Blanks—Two points each
Directions: On the lines provided, write the best answer.

1. When Merlyn sends Arthur and Kay on an adventure in the Forest Sauvage, they meet

_____

2. When they arrive at Castle Chariot, it seems to be made of _____

3. When Merlyn transforms Arthur into an ant, Arthur discovers that ants have only two ways of

describing things: _____ and _____

4. When Arthur, as a wild goose, suggests to Lyo-Lyok that geese fight each other, she becomes

_____

5. When Kay forgets his sword for the tournament in London, Arthur brings him _____

_____

6. In order to create a small magic to become invisible, Morgause _____

_____

7. In order to eliminate jealousy among his new order of knights, Arthur proposes that they all

_____

8. Physically, Lancelot can be described as _____

9. Lancelot's most prized possession was his _____

10. Lancelot falls in love with Guenever because he has _____

11. Morgause, like the unicorn, is killed by _____

12. After returning from the Quest for the Grail, Lancelot refuses to be Guenever's lover again because

_____

13. When she finally realizes that Lancelot will never stay with her as her husband, Elaine

_____

14. Sir Urre can only have his wounds healed by_____and the one who does this is

_____

15. As a result of having Lancelot caught in her room, Guenever is sentenced to be _____

16. While Arthur and Gawaine are in France fighting Lancelot, Mordred plans to spread the lie that

_____

17. Mordred also plans to marry _____

18. When Quenever blockades herself in the Tower of London, Mordred attacks the Tower with

_____

19. In the Justice Room at Camelot there are tapestries representing the Bible story of _____

_____

20. In talking to Tom, his page, before the battle of Salisbury, Arthur compares his ideal to

_____

Part 3—Short Essays—Three points each
Directions: Answer in two or three sentences.

1. Name one way T.H. White makes fun of customs of the Middle Ages as described in books like Malory's.

2. What lesson does Arthur learn from his transformation into an ant?

3. Name one thing Arthur learns from his adventure with Robin Hood in the Forest Sauvage.

4. What was Arthur's original ideal?

5. What are the young Lancelot's attitudes and emotions concerning Arthur and his ideal?

6. What part did God play in the Eternal Quadrangle which pulls Lancelot apart?

7. Why does Arthur initiate the Quest for the Grail?

8. Why can the Quest for the Grail be considered a failure?

9. Why does Arthur forbid Lancelot to kill Mordred?

10. How can Arthur's review of his life at the end of the novel be considered both optimistic and pessimistic?

Answer Key—Quizzes

Quiz 1

1. d   2. a   3. b   4. c   5. b   6. d   7. c   8. a   9. b   10. b

Quiz 2

1. c   2. b   3. a   4. c   5. a   6. b   7. d   8. c   9. a   10. d

Quiz 3

1. d   2. a   3. c   4. b   5. a   6. b   7. c   8. d   9. b   10. b   11. a   12. c   13. d
14. a   15. d   16. True   17. True   18. False   19. False   20. True

Quiz 4

1. b   2. a   3. c   4. d   5. c   6. a   7. d   8. b   9. c   10. d

Quiz 5

1. b   2. b   3. a   4. c   5. d   6. a   7. c   8. c   9. d   10. b

Quiz 6

1. c   2. d   3. a   4. b   5. d   6. a   7. b   8. c   9. a   10. c   11. b   12. c   13. d
14. b   15. a   16. False   17. True   18. True   19. False   20. True

Answer Key—Final Test

Part 1

1. Q	6. K	11. B	16. I
2. W	7. N	12. Z	17. S
3. E	8. T	13. V	18. G
4. R	9. J	14. Y	19. C
5. A	10. P	15. H	20. M

Part 2

1. Robin Hood and his men

2. food

3. Done and Not Done

4. angry and upset

5. the sword in the stone

6. boils a live cat

7. sit at a round table

8. ugly

9. word

10. hurt her

11. Agravaine

12. he has seen God

13. kills herself

14. the best knight in the world/Lancelot

15. burned at the stake

16. Lancelot and Arthur are dead

17. Guenever

18. cannon

19. David and Bathsheba or Susannah and the elders

20. a candle in the wind

Bibliography
The New Matter of Britain:
Contemporary Arthurian Literature

I. Source Material

Barber, Richard, ed. *The Arthurian Legends: An Illustrated Anthology.* Totowa: Littlefield Adams and Co., 1979.

Benson, Larry D., ed. *King Arthur's Death.* Indianapolis: Bobbs-Merrill, 1974.

Beroul, *The Romance of Tristan.* Trans. Alan S. Fedrick. Harmondsworth, England: Penguin, 1971.

The Death of King Arthur. Trans. James Cable. Harmondsworth, England: Penguin, 1971.

de Troyes, Chretien. *Arthurian Romances.* Trans. W.W. Comfort. New York: Dutton's Everyman Library, 1975.

Geoffrey of Monmouth. *History of the Kings of Britain.* Trans. Sebastian Evans. New York: E.P. Dutton, 1958.

The Mabinogion. Trans. Jeffery Ganz. Harmondsworth, England: Penguin, 1976.

Malory, Sir Thomas. *Le Morte D'Arthur: A New Rendition by Keith Baines.* New York: Bramhall House, 1962.

_____. *Tales of King Arthur.* Edited and abridged by Michael Senior. New York: Schocken Books, 1980.

The Quest of the Holy Grail. Trans. P.M. Montarasso. Harmondsworth, England: Penguin, 1969.

Sir Gawaine and the Green Knight. Trans. P.M. Brian Stone. Baltimore: Penguin, 1959.

Von Eschenbach, Wolfram. *Parzival.* Trans. Helen M. Mustard and Charles E. Passage. New York: Random House Vintage Books, 1961.

Von Strassburg, Gottfried. *Tristan.* Trans. A. T. Hatto. Harmondsworth, England: Penguin, 1960.

Wace and Layamon. *Arthurian Charonicles.* Trans. Eugene Mason. New York: Dutton's Everyman Library, 1962.

II. Background and Analysis of Arthurian Material

Alcock, Leslie. *Arthur's Britian.* Harmondsworth, England: Penguin, 1971.

Apone, Carl. "In Search of Camleot," *The Pittsburgh Press Roto Magazine,* Sunday, January 20, 1980, pp 8ff.

Ashe, Geoffrey. *Avalonian Quest.* London: Fontana Paperbacks, 1984.

_____. *Camelot and the Vision of Albion.* London: William Heinmann, 1971.

_____. *A Guidebook to Arthurian Britian.* Wellingborough, England: The Aquarian Press, 1983.

_____. *King Arthur's Avalon: The Story of Glastonbury.* Glasgow: Collins Fontana Books, 1957.

_____. ed. *The Quest for Arthur's Britian.* London: Granada Paladin Book, 1971.

Ashton, Graham. *The Realm of King Arthur.* Newport, Isle of Wight: J. Arthur Dixon, 1974.

Baxter, Sylvester. *The Legend of the Holy Grail.* Boston: Curtis and Cameron, 1904.

Cavendish, Richard. *King Arthur and the Grail: The Arthurian Romances.* New York: Taplinger Publishing Company, 1978.

Darrah, John. *The Real Camelot: Paganism and the Arthurian Romances.* New York: Thames and Hudson, 1981.

Herm, Gerhard. *The Celts: The People Who Came Out of the Darkness.* New York: St. Martin's Press, 1977.

Holbrook, Sabra. *Sir Tristan of All Time.* New York: Ferrar, Straus and Giroux, 1970.

Holiday Film Corporation. *The Story of King Arthur. A Sound-Slide Presentation.* Whittier, California: Holiday Film Corporation, 1983.

Hoskins, Richard. *Westward to Arthur.* Lizard Town, England: Pendragon House U.K. Ltd., 1978.

Howard-Gordon, Frances. *Glastonbury: Maker of Myths.* Glastonbury: Gothic Image 1982.

Jenkins, Elizabeth. *The Mystery of King Arthur.* New York: Coward, McCann and Geoghegan, 1975.

Karr, Phyllis Ann. *The King Arthur Companion.* Reston, Virginia: Reston Publishing Co., Inc., 1983.

Knight, Gareth. *The Secret Tradition in Arthurian Legend.* Wellingborough, England: The Aquarian Press, 1983.

Matthews, John. *The Grail: The Quest for the Eternal.* London: Thames and Hudson Ltd., 1981.

Morris, John. *The Age of Arthur.* New York: Scribners, 1973.

Nitze, William Albert. *Arthurian Romance and Modern Poetry and Music.* Port Washington, New York: Kennikat Press, 1970.

Radford, C. A. Raleigh and Michael J. Swanton. *Arthurian Sites in the West.* Devon, England: University of Exeter, 1975.

Taylor, Beverley and Elizabeth Brewer. *The Return of King Arthur: British and American Arthurian Literature Since 1800.* Woodbridge, Suffolk, England: D.S. Brewer, 1983.

Turner, Barbara Carpenter. *King Arthur and the Round Table.* Winchester and London: Gabare Ltd., 1979.

West Country Tourist Board. *The Land of Legend.* Exeter: Sydney Lee Ltd., 1978.

Weston, Jesse L. *From Ritual to Romance.* Garden City: Double Anchor, 1957.

Wettengel, Thomas. Under the direction of Leo Kneer and Nora Rotzoll and in consultation with Leslie Alcock. *These Halls of Camelot.* Glenview, Illinois: Scott, Foresman and Company, 1972.

III. Novels and Retellings of the Legend

Berger, Thomas. *Arthur Rex.* New York: Delacorte Press, 1978.

Bradley, Marion Zimmer. *The Mists of Avalon.* New York: Alfred A. Knopf, 1982.

Bradshaw, Gillian. *Hawk of May.* New York: Simon and Schuster, 1980.

_____. *In Winter's Shadow.* New York: Simon and Schuster, 1981.

_____. *The Kingdom of Summer.* New York: Simon and Schuster, 1981.

Canning, Victor. *The Crimson Chalice.* New York: William Morrow and Company Inc., 1978.

Chant, Joy. *The High Kings: Arthur's Celtic Ancestors.* Toronto: Bantam Books, 1983.

Chapman, Graham et al. *Monty Python and the Holy Grail (Book)*. New York: Methuen, Inc., 1977.

Chapman, Vera. *The Green Knight*. New York: Avon, 1975.

_____. *King Arthur's Daughter*. New York: Avon, 1976.

_____. *The King's Damsel*. New York: Avon, 1976.

Christian, Catherine. *The Pendragon*. New York: Alfred A. Knopf, 1979.

Drake, David. *The Dragon Lord*. New York:TOR A Tom Doherty Associates Book, 1982.

Duggan, Alfred. *Conscience of the King*. London: Peter Davies, 1976.

Godwin, Parke. *Beloved Exile: A Novel of Guenevere*. Toronto: Bantam Books, 1984.

_____. *Firelord*. Garden City, New York: Doubleday and Company Inc., 1980.

Green, Roger Lancelyn. *King Arthur and His Knights of the Round Table*. Harmondsworth, England: Puffin Books, 1953.

Johnson, Barbara Ferry. *Lionors*. New York: Avon, 1975.

Jones, Gwyn. *Welsh Legends and Folktales*. Harmondsworth, England: Puffin Books, 1979.

Kane, Gil and John Jakes, *Excalibur!*. New York: Dell, 1980.

Karr Phyllis Ann. *The Idylls of the Queen*. New York: Ace Books, 1982.

Monaco, Richard. *The Final Quest*. New York: Macmillan, 1980.

_____. *The Grail War*. New York: Macmillan, 1979.

_____. *Parsival or A Knight's Tale*. New York: Macmillan, 1977.

Newman, Sharan. *The Chessboard Queen*. New York: St. Martin's Press, 1983.

_____. *Guinevere. New York: St. Martin's Press*, 1981.

Norton, Andre. *Merlin's Mirror*. New York: Daw, 1975.

Nye, Robert. *Merlin*. New York: G. P. Putnam's Sons, 1979.

Ponsor, Y. R. *Gawaine and the Green Knight: Adventure at Camelot*. New York: Macmillan, 1979.

Roberts, Dorothy James. *The Enchanted Cup*. New York: Appleton-Century-Crofts, Inc., 1953.

_____. *Lancelot, My Brother*. New York: Appleton-Century-Crofts, Inc., 1954.

Seare, Nicholas, *Rude Tales and Glorious: A Retelling of the Arthurian Tales*. New York: Clarkson H. Potter Inc., 1983.

Steinbeck, John. *The Acts of King Arthur and His Noble Knights*. New York: Avenel Books, 1982.

Stewart, Mary. *The Merlin Trilogy* (containing *The Crystal Cave, The Hollow Hills* and *The Last Enchantment*). New York: William Morrow and Company Inc., 1980.

_____. *The Wicked Day*. New York: William Morrow and Company Inc., 1983.

Sutcliff, Rosemary. *The Light Beyond the Forest*. London: Hodder and Stoughton Knight Books, 1979.

_____. *The Road to Camlann*. London: Hodder and Stoughton Knight Books, 1984.

_____. *The Sword and the Circle*. London: Hodder and Stoughton Knight Books, 1981.

_____. *Sword at Sunset.* London: Hodder and Stoughton, 1963.

Tennyson, Alfred Lord. *Idylls of the King.* New York: New American Library Signet Classic, 1961.

Treece, Henry. *The Great Captains.* Manchester, England: Savoy Books, New English Library, 1980.

Twain, Mark. (Samuel L. Clemens). *A Connecticut Yankee in King Arthur's Court.* New York: Washington Square Press Pocket Books, 1948.

Weeks, Stephen and Henry Whittington. *Sword of the Valiant: The Legend of Sir Gawaine and the Green Knight.* London: Sphere Books Limited, 1984.

White, T.H. *The Book of Merlyn.* New York: Berkeley Publishing Company, 1977.

_____. *The Once and Future King.* New York: G.P. Putmnam's Sons, 1958.

Williams, Charles and C. S. Lewis. *Taliessin Through Logres, The Region of Summer Stars, and Arthurian Torso.* Grand Rapids: William B. Eerdmans Publishing Company, 1974.

Acknowledgments

For permission to reprint all works in this volume, grateful acknowlegment is made to the following holders of copyright, publishers, or representatives.

Lesson 2, Handout 5, and Lesson 4, Handout 17
Excerpts from *Tales of King Arthur* by Sir Thomas Malory, edited and abridged by Michael Senior, Reprinted by permission of Schocken Books. Published by Pantheon Books, a Division of Random House, Inc.

Lesson 6, Handout 25
C'EST MOI by Alan Jay Lerner & Frederick Loewe. Copyright (c) 1960 by Alan Jay Lerner & Frederick Loewe. All Rights Administered by Chappell & Co., Inc. International Copyright Secured. All Rights Reserved. Used by permission.

Lesson 9, Handout 37
Excerpt from *The Once and Future King* by T. H. White. Reprinted by permission of the Putnam Publishing Group, Copyright (c) 1939, 1940, 1958 by T. H. White.

Lesson 10, Handout 39
Excerpt from *One Brief Shining Moment: Remembering Kennedy* by William Manchester, 1983. Published by Little, Brown & Co., Boston, Massachusetts.

NOVEL/DRAMA

CURRICULUM UNITS

Novel/Drama Series

Novel

*Absolutely Normal Chaos/
Chasing Redbird*, Creech

Across Five Aprils, Hunt

Adam of the Road, Gray/*Catherine,
Called Birdy*, Cushman

*The Adventures of Huckleberry
Finn*, Twain

The Adventures of Tom Sawyer,
Twain

*Alice's Adventures in Wonderland/
Through the Looking-Glass*,
Carroll

All Creatures Great and Small,
Herriot

All Quiet on the Western Front,
Remarque

All the King's Men, Warren

Animal Farm, Orwell/
The Book of the Dun Cow,
Wangerin, Jr.

Anna Karenina, Tolstoy

*Anne Frank: The Diary of a Young
Girl*, Frank

Anne of Green Gables, Montgomery

April Morning, Fast

The Assistant/The Fixer, Malamud

*The Autobiography of Miss Jane
Pittman*, Gaines

The Awakening, Chopin/
Madame Bovary, Flaubert

Babbitt, Lewis

The Bean Trees/Pigs in Heaven,
Kingsolver

Beowulf/Grendel, Gardner

Billy Budd/Moby Dick, Melville

Black Boy, Wright

Bless Me, Ultima, Anaya

Brave New World, Huxley

The Bridge of San Luis Rey, Wilder

The Brothers Karamazov,
Dostoevsky

The Call of the Wild/White Fang,
London

The Canterbury Tales, Chaucer

The Catcher in the Rye, Salinger

The Cay/Timothy of the Cay, Taylor

Charlotte's Web, White/
The Secret Garden, Burnett

The Chosen, Potok

The Christmas Box, Evans/
A Christmas Carol, Dickens

Chronicles of Narnia, Lewis

Cold Mountain, Frazier

Cold Sassy Tree, Burns

*The Color of Water: A Black Man's
Tribute to His White Mother*,
McBride

The Count of Monte Cristo, Dumas

Crime and Punishment, Dostoevsky

Cry, the Beloved Country, Paton

Dandelion Wine, Bradbury

Darkness at Noon, Koestler

David Copperfield, Dickens

Davita's Harp, Potok

A Day No Pigs Would Die, Peck

Death Comes for the Archbishop,
Cather

December Stillness, Hahn/
Izzy, Willy-Nilly, Voigt

The Divine Comedy, Dante

The Dollmaker, Arnow

Don Quixote, Cervantes

Dr. Zhivago, Pasternak

Dubliners, Joyce

East of Eden, Steinbeck

The Egypt Game, Snyder/
The Bronze Bow, Speare

Ellen Foster/A Virtuous Woman,
Gibbons

Emma, Austen

Fahrenheit 451, Bradbury

A Farewell to Arms, Hemingway

Farewell to Manzanar, Houston &
Houston/*Black Like Me*, Griffin

Frankenstein, Shelley

*From the Mixed-up Files of Mrs.
Basil E. Frankweiler*,
Konigsburg/*The Westing Game*,
Raskin

A Gathering of Flowers, Thomas, ed.

The Giver, Lowry

The Good Earth, Buck

The Grapes of Wrath, Steinbeck

Great Expectations, Dickens

The Great Gatsby, Fitzgerald

Gulliver's Travels, Swift

Hard Times, Dickens

Hatchet, Paulsen/*Robinson Crusoe*,
Defoe

Having Our Say, Delany, Delany, and
Hearth/*A Gathering of Old
Men*, Gaines

The Heart Is a Lonely Hunter,
McCullers

Heart of Darkness, Conrad

Hiroshima, Hersey/*On the Beach*,
Shute

The Hobbit, Tolkien

Homecoming/Dicey's Song, Voigt

The Hound of the Baskervilles,
Doyle

*The Human Comedy/
My Name Is Aram*, Saroyan

Incident at Hawk's Hill, Eckert/
Where the Red Fern Grows,
Rawls

Invisible Man, Ellison

Jane Eyre, Brontë

Johnny Tremain, Forbes

Journey of the Sparrows, Buss and
Cubias/*The Honorable Prison*, de
Jenkins

The Joy Luck Club, Tan

Jubal Sackett/The Walking Drum,
L'Amour

Julie of the Wolves, George/*Island
of the Blue Dolphins*, O'Dell

The Jungle, Sinclair

The Killer Angels, Shaara

Le Morte D'Arthur, Malory

The Learning Tree, Parks

Les Miserables, Hugo

*The Light in the Forest/
A Country of Strangers*, Richter

*Little House in the Big Woods/
Little House on the Prairie*,
Wilder

Little Women, Alcott

Lord of the Flies, Golding

The Lord of the Rings, Tolkien

The Martian Chronicles, Bradbury

Missing May, Rylant/*The Summer
of the Swans*, Byars

Mrs. Mike, Freedman/*I Heard the
Owl Call My Name*, Craven

*Murder on the Orient Express/
And Then There Were None*,
Christie

My Antonia, Cather

The Natural, Malamud/*Shoeless
Joe*, Kinsella

Nectar in a Sieve, Markandaya/
The Woman Warrior, Kingston

Night, Wiesel

A Night to Remember, Lord/*Streams
to the River, River to the Sea*,
O'Dell

1984, Orwell

Number the Stars, Lowry/*Friedrich*,
Richter

Obasan, Kogawa

The Odyssey, Homer

The Old Man and the Sea,
Hemingway/*Ethan Frome*,
Wharton

The Once and Future King, White

O Pioneers!, Cather/*The Country of
the Pointed Firs*, Jewett

Ordinary People, Guest/
  The Tin Can Tree, Tyler

The Outsiders, Hinton/
  Durango Street, Bonham

The Pearl/Of Mice and Men,
  Steinbeck

The Picture of Dorian Gray, Wilde/
  Dr. Jekyll and Mr. Hyde,
  Stevenson

The Pigman/The Pigman's Legacy,
  Zindel

The Poisonwood Bible, Kingsolver

*A Portrait of the Artist as a Young
  Man*, Joyce

The Power and the Glory, Greene

A Prayer for Owen Meany, Irving

Pride and Prejudice, Austen

The Prince, Machiavelli/*Utopia*,
  More

The Prince and the Pauper, Twain

Profiles in Courage, Kennedy

Rebecca, du Maurier

The Red Badge of Courage, Crane

Red Sky at Morning, Bradford

The Return of the Native, Hardy

A River Runs Through It, Maclean

*Roll of Thunder, Hear My Cry/
  Let the Circle Be Unbroken*,
  Taylor

Saint Maybe, Tyler

Sarum, Rutherfurd

The Scarlet Letter, Hawthorne

The Scarlet Pimpernel, Orczy

A Separate Peace, Knowles

*Shabanu: Daughter of the Wind/
  Haveli*, Staples

Shane, Schaefer/*The Ox-Bow
  Incident*, Van Tilburg Clark

Siddhartha, Hesse

*The Sign of the Chrysanthemum/
  The Master Puppeteer*, Paterson

*The Signet Classic Book of Southern
  Short Stories*, Abbott and
  Koppelman, eds.

Silas Marner, Eliot/*The Elephant
  Man*, Sparks

The Slave Dancer, Fox/
  I, Juan de Pareja, De Treviño

Snow Falling on Cedars, Guterson

Song of Solomon, Morrison

The Sound and the Fury, Faulkner

Spoon River Anthology, Masters

*A Stranger Is Watching/I'll Be
  Seeing You*, Higgins Clark

The Stranger/The Plague, Camus

Summer of My German Soldier,
  Greene/*Waiting for the Rain*,
  Gordon

A Tale of Two Cities, Dickens

Talking God/A Thief of Time,
  Hillerman

Tara Road/The Return Journey,
  Binchy

Tess of the D'Urbervilles, Hardy

Their Eyes Were Watching God,
  Hurston

*Things Fall Apart/No Longer at
  Ease*, Achebe

To Kill a Mockingbird, Lee

To the Lighthouse, Woolf

Travels with Charley, Steinbeck

Treasure Island, Stevenson

A Tree Grows in Brooklyn, Smith

Tuck Everlasting, Babbitt/
  Bridge to Terabithia, Paterson

The Turn of the Screw/Daisy Miller,
  James

Uncle Tom's Cabin, Stowe

The Unvanquished, Faulkner

Walden, Thoreau/*A Different
  Drummer*, Kelley

Walk Two Moons, Creech

Walkabout, Marshall

Watership Down, Adams

*The Watsons Go to Birmingham—
  1963*, Curtis/*The View from
  Saturday*, Konigsburg

When the Legends Die, Borland

Where the Lilies Bloom, Cleaver/
  No Promises in the Wind, Hunt

Winesburg, Ohio, Anderson

The Witch of Blackbird Pond,
  Speare/*My Brother Sam Is Dead*,
  Collier and Collier

A Wrinkle in Time, L'Engle/*The
  Lion, the Witch and the Ward-
  robe*, Lewis

Wuthering Heights, Brontë

The Yearling, Rawlings/
  The Red Pony, Steinbeck

Year of Impossible Goodbyes, Choi/
  So Far from the Bamboo Grove,
  Watkins

Zlata's Diary, Filipović/
  The Lottery Rose, Hunt

Drama

Antigone, Sophocles

Arms and the Man/Saint Joan,
  Shaw

The Crucible, Miller

Cyrano de Bergerac, Rostand

Death of a Salesman, Miller

A Doll's House/Hedda Gabler, Ibsen

The Glass Menagerie, Williams

The Importance of Being Earnest,
  Wilde

Inherit the Wind, Lawrence and Lee

Long Day's Journey into Night,
  O'Neill

A Man for All Seasons, Bolt

Medea, Euripides/*The Lion in
  Winter*, Goldman

The Miracle Worker, Gibson

Murder in the Cathedral, Eliot/
  Galileo, Brecht

The Night Thoreau Spent in Jail,
  Lawrence and Lee

Oedipus the King, Sophocles

Our Town, Wilder

*The Playboy of the Western World/
  Riders to the Sea*, Synge

Pygmalion, Shaw

A Raisin in the Sun, Hansberry

1776, Stone and Edwards

She Stoops to Conquer, Goldsmith/
  The Matchmaker, Wilder

A Streetcar Named Desire, Williams

Tara Road/The Return Journey,
  Binchy

Tartuffe, Molière

*Three Comedies of American Family
  Life: I Remember Mama*, van
  Druten/*Life with Father*, Lindsay
  and Crouse/*You Can't Take It
  with You*, Hart and Kaufman

Waiting for Godot, Beckett/
  *Rosencrantz & Guildenstern Are
  Dead*, Stoppard

Shakespeare

As You Like It

Hamlet

Henry IV, Part I

Henry V

Julius Caesar

King Lear

Macbeth

The Merchant of Venice

A Midsummer Night's Dream

Much Ado about Nothing

Othello

Richard III

Romeo and Juliet

The Taming of the Shrew

The Tempest

Twelfth Night

The Center for Learning

To Order Contact: **The Center for Learning—Shipping/Business Office**
P.O. Box 910 • Villa Maria, PA 16155
800-767-9090 • 724-964-8083 • Fax 888-767-8080

The Publisher

All instructional materials identified by the TAP® (Teachers/Authors/Publishers) trademark are developed by a national network of teachers whose collective educational experience distinguishes the publishing objective of The Center for Learning, a nonprofit educational corporation founded in 1970.

Concentrating on values-related disciplines, the Center publishes humanities and religion curriculum units for use in public and private schools and other educational settings. Approximately 500 language arts, social studies, novel/drama, life issues, and faith publications are available.

While acutely aware of the challenges and uncertain solutions to growing educational problems, the Center is committed to quality curriculum development and to the expansion of learning opportunities for all students. Publications are regularly evaluated and updated to meet the changing and diverse needs of teachers and students. Teachers may offer suggestions for development of new publications or revisions of existing titles by contacting

The Center for Learning

Administrative/Editorial Office
21590 Center Ridge Rd.
Rocky River, OH 44116
(440) 331-1404 • FAX (440) 331-5414
E-mail: cfl@stratos.net
Web: www.centerforlearning.org

For a free catalog containing order and price information and a descriptive listing of titles, contact

The Center for Learning

Shipping/Business Office
P.O. Box 910
Villa Maria, PA 16155
(724) 964-8083 • (800) 767-9090
FAX (888) 767-8080